CW01631834

# Troubled Waters

MARY JONES

Beleura Hill

First published 2020

Beleura Hill Books
PO Box 435
Mornington
VIC
3931
Australia



ISBN 978-0-9873074-4-6

Book design by Philip Jones
Cover illustration from a photograph by Rosy Ritter-Jones (footprints courtesy of Bailey McLellan).

Mary Jones migrated to Australia in November 2008 from England, where she was a member of The Writers' Guild of Great Britain and The Crime Writers' Association. She had short stories published in magazines in the UK, Scandinavia and South Africa, and one broadcast on BBC Radio 4. She worked extensively in amateur theatre in the UK, as writer, director and actor, and has had full-length stage scripts performed by both amateurs and professionals.

Since moving to Australia she has continued to write fiction, playscripts and poetry. Her work has been published in magazines and anthologies, awarded competition prizes, performed on radio and set to music. She has four published collections of poetry. *Troubled Waters* is her first novel.

*Poetry by Mary Jones :*

Lines Dancing
(Beleura Hill, 2012)

Second Person Singular
(Ginninderra Press Pocket Poets Series, 2016)

Lines Waving
(Beleura Hill, 2017)

Cast of Supporting Characters
(Ginninderra Press Pocket Poets Series, 2018)

*www.maryjonesthewriter.com*

# PROLOGUE

## MARCH 1945

The evening was cold; the air still and cloudless. Hugo paused halfway down the cliff path and stood looking out over the sea below. He listened to the gentle lapping of the incoming tide, and the sound of voices drifting across the beach from the island's barracks at Fort Le Cocq. Shimmering silver fingers of water were already creeping out towards the lowest sections of the causeway leading to it; soon the fort would be completely cut off.

The voices were subdued, and the light from the windows flickered feebly. Hugo thought of his men in their threadbare uniforms, huddled round the single oil lamp in the guard room. He hugged to himself the memory of the warm barn he'd just left; the steam rising from the flanks of the gentle-eyed cattle and the comfort of hand-knitted wool on his skin.

He was about to continue down the path when a movement caught his eye, beneath the main wall of the fort. A dark figure was moving across the rocks to skirt the guard room and come out on to the causeway below it. He stood watching until the figure had reached the centre of the causeway, picking its way through the water already beginning to swirl gently across the path.

He was still trying to decide whether to turn back to avoid the figure or go on to accost it when the sky exploded. The first blast was followed by a few seconds of uncanny silence, then the air was full of the sounds of shells bursting and the crackle of cartridges, the crash of falling masonry and the screams of men crushed and burning.

He knew at once what had happened. Whether by accident or design, the ammunition store had blown up. Stumbling and cursing, Hugo began to run down the path.

## JULY 1985

The clear path of moonlight across the bay began to waver and crinkle as a breeze stirred the surface of the water. Soon its edges were lost, broken up into fragments by the movement of developing waves and the stir of tidal currents from below. Sometimes it disappeared altogether as clouds scudded across the moon.

A row of pink floats along the edge of the headland swirled and bobbed in the eddies formed by the turning tide. A watcher from the cliff-top path might have wondered at the sudden violence of their movement. But there was no watcher; no sound except the lap of the waves on the beach and the whispering of the rising wind; no light as the clouds gathered and deepened.

In silence and darkness, the body broke the surface and settled into the embrace of weed-covered rope.

# CHAPTER 1

## JULY 1985

'Who wants this?'

'Me!'

There were several voices eager to claim the Walkman that Dominic Henderson waved above his head, but Robbie Martel's was the first, and the loudest. He caught it deftly as it was tossed casually across the room to him.

'You're crazy, Henderson! Why on earth do you want to throw this out? It looks brand new.'

Henderson shrugged.

'Doesn't work.'

'It probably just needs new batteries, you wally. I bet you haven't even checked.'

'Can't be bothered,' agreed Henderson. 'You can do that, and see if it's worth mending. Mum will just buy me a new one.'

Robbie had met Henderson's mother, and he knew it was

true. Her darling Dominic could do no wrong, and must have everything he wanted as soon as he wanted it. Pity she couldn't buy him intelligence, but she did buy him just about everything else.

'O.K. – if you're sure. Thanks, Henderson.'

For a few minutes the end-of-term clearing up of the school boarding-house common-room proceeded in relative quiet. Then a different voice rang out.

'Anyone want this?'

'Oh, come off it, Lovering, you've got to be joking. Who in his right mind would want one grotty games sock?'

'Someone who's got an odd one to match it with, of course,' said Lovering calmly, ignoring the ribald comments and nose-holding gestures around him. '*I've* got a spare pair. Come on, everybody. Any takers? You wouldn't even have to come and get it. It would probably walk over to you all by itself!'

'Don't be revolting, Lovering,' said Henderson, 'just ditch the beastly thing. The bin's over there.'

Robbie caught Lovering's eye, and they chorused together,

'Bin there; done that!'

'But not got the tee-shirt,' added Robbie, 'tee-shirts are *much* too vulgar for Henderson.'

He heard the other boys snigger and knew he was being mean, taking a rise out of Henderson. But it was so easy – half the time Henderson never even realised when he was being got at. And he *did* go on and on about all the exotic places he'd been to on holiday.

'Where are you going this time, Henderson?' asked Lovering, 'The Bahamas?'

'The Seychelles, actually,' said Henderson smugly, 'Everybody does the Bahamas these days.'

'Oh, of course. Silly me!' said Robbie, 'How could I have forgotten that the Bahamas are outré this season?' He wasn't absolutely sure what outré meant; he had a nasty feeling it was probably the opposite of what he wanted it to mean. Perhaps he should have said passé. Never mind – it was a dead cert that Henderson wouldn't know the difference.

The sniggering broke out again, and this time even Henderson couldn't miss it. He might not be all that bright, but he wasn't totally insensitive. He flushed, and lumbered to the attack.

'It's all very well making snide remarks, Martel, but I bet you're just jealous.'

Robbie grinned.

'Jealous of the Seychelles? Don't make me laugh. I've got my own island, thanks.'

'Yes, so I've heard. You always go off on some pathetic cheap package trip to the Channel Islands, don't you? And not even Jersey, either, just one of the deadbeat small islands nobody's even heard of.'

Lovering leapt to his friend's defence.

'That just shows what a fat lot you know about it. He doesn't need to go on any stupid package. His parents own the whole island, *actually*.'

Robbie enjoyed enormously the expression on Henderson's face, but since he was essentially a truthful boy he felt bound to put the record straight.

'Well, no – they don't *own* it exactly. But my father does run the whole island. My parents are the tenants, you see. The island's leased from Guernsey.'

'Oh, well ... Tenants!' said Henderson scornfully, going back to his packing, and Robbie wished he'd held his tongue.

'Which island is it?' asked Addenbrooke, a small red-haired boy whose face was a mass of freckles. 'I think my parents might have gone there once. I know it was a small island, and they had to get to it from Guernsey, but I can't remember what it was called.'

'Ours is Longuey,' said Robbie, strangely reluctant to talk about it. 'Bigger than Herm, smaller than Sark.'

*And better than both of them,* he thought but didn't say aloud.

'That was it,' said Addenbrooke, 'Longuey. I remember now. My father said it was bloody boring. It rained most of the time and there was nothing to do.'

Robbie said nothing, but concentrated on clearing out his locker. He was glad Mr. Addenbrooke had found Longuey boring – that meant they wouldn't be back.

As far as Robbie was concerned, a large part of the magic of his island was that it *didn't* appeal to obnoxious characters like the Addenbrookes and the Hendersons.

* * *

Neville Blythe leaned back against the green leather of the Government backbenches, and allowed himself the luxury of a few minutes' relaxation. The tricky moment had passed, and the rest of the debate should now be comfortably boring. Nothing the Minister couldn't handle quite competently for himself, without the need for any further input from his junior colleague.

The progress of the debate had followed the usual pattern: opening statement by the Minister for the Environment; attacking statement by his shadow in the Opposition, combining valid points with wild exaggeration and genteel insults; reply by the Minister, not answering any of the points raised but quoting the amount of money spent by the Government, and returning the insults with equal gentility to appreciative laughter from his own benches. Honours even so far; the Minister and his shadow had both graduated in the art of exquisite insolence from the same public school.

The following backbench contributions also ran largely true to form, with no opportunity missed by either side to score party political points and hurl blame across the floor of the House. A sole Liberal Democrat attempted to ask a sensible question about renewable energy, and was wiped out by a cheap crack about tilting at windmills. The contributions from pre-primed Government supporters went well, the rhetorical questions fulfilling their intended function of leading into already prepared ministerial replies.

The awkward moment had come unexpectedly, as an Opposition member caught the Speaker's eye and rose to deliver a short but telling speech which managed the rare combination of passion, relevance and dignity. Neville saw at once that the Minister was rattled, shuffling the papers on his lap and hesitating for a moment rather than leaping to the Dispatch Box to reply immediately. Without waiting for a nod from the Speaker, he rose himself and came smoothly to the rescue.

'Would my honourable friend agree ...'

The Minister recovered from his momentary discomfiture, and his normal suavity reasserted itself as he took Neville's reply and elaborated on it. He gave no direct sign, by glance or inclination of the head, of acknowledgement of the rescue, but it had been noted.

Not for nothing was Neville Blythe known in the House of Commons tearooms as 'The Lifebelt'. His talent for extricating himself and others from potentially awkward situations had not yet resulted in a Cabinet post, but it could surely only be a matter of time.

Now the immediate danger was past. Opposition members, who would have been baying for blood if the Minister had faltered, lapsed into muttered conversation and the occasional yawn as he swung into his well rehearsed summing up. Soon the live television coverage would be over for the day, and any further problems could be safely dealt with in committee, away from public scrutiny.

Neville drew a voluptuously convoluted doodle on the edge of his order paper, and stared appraisingly at the only female member of the Shadow Cabinet present, on the front bench opposite him. He often deplored, both privately and in public, the fact that even the most attractive women in the House tended to wear staid and unprovocative suits, usually in unflattering primary colours. Still, at least this one sported high heels, and she had excellent ankles.

He lapsed into daydreams of other, younger ankles, and the legs that went with them, and the body that went with the legs. Unfortunately, the mind and will that went with the body were likely to test to the full even *his* powers of damage limitation. He prided himself on his ability to live dangerously, but he was forced to admit in his saner moments that this time he'd bitten off rather more than he could safely hope to chew. Getting heavily involved with the daughter of the Foreign Secretary was foolhardy enough; when the daughter had been quietly requested not to return to Cambridge to begin her second year because of a drug involvement that hadn't come to court, it began to look suicidal.

He knew the sensible thing to do would be to ditch Abigail as fast as possible, but when had he ever done the sensible thing? Sensible responses to problems were for pathetic little Liberal Democrats, who got destroyed by anybody with an ounce of flair. He thought again of Abby's body, and what she could do with it, and he knew the danger was part of the attraction. She undoubtedly caused problems, but she contributed her own flair to the search for solutions. Her gift for improvisation almost matched his own, and he sometimes wondered whether her talent for deception actually surpassed his. The web of deceit they'd concocted to engineer their coming holiday together was beautiful in its complexity, plugging every possible loophole. Only one more week of this tedious debate and committee work, and he'd be free to savour all the talents Cambridge had failed to appreciate. Typical of Cambridge not to recognise quality when they saw it. He was an Oxford man himself.

He drew out of his briefcase the hotel brochure that had come with the confirmation of his holiday booking. He hardly needed to remind himself of most of the details, as he had spent a large proportion of each Summer Recess at Longuey for the last five years, though not always with the same companions. Nevertheless, there were some changes in this year's brochure that interested him particularly. With the meticulous attention to detail that had been such an asset to him in his parliamentary career to date, he began to compare the current brochure with the one he had kept from last year.

* * *

'I'll make us a nice pot of tea then, shall I dear?'

Jean looked at the still-warm teapot on the table beside her and sighed.

'All right, Mum, you do that.'

'I'll do that, then, shall I? I'll just go out and put the kettle on. Won't be a minute.' Muriel shuffled out to the kitchen.

Jean opened the folder marked 'Holiday' and spread the contents out on the table. Brian had said it would be fine to go ahead with all the arrangements, but Jean was beginning to worry. Mum had been getting so much worse lately, even in the familiar surroundings of home. Brian was very good with her, of course, but he didn't know the full story – how could he, when he was out at work all day? She'd tried to tell him how bad things were getting, but she didn't want to sound whining and resentful. As it was, he thought she was exaggerating. Muriel was never as bad when he was at home, somehow. In her more lucid moments, they even joked about it.

'She's always on her best behaviour for me, aren't you, Mu?'

'Must behave myself for my daughter's best boy.' Then with a sly look at Jean, 'I promised.'

It was true. She'd been a dragon with Jean's previous boyfriends; a fiercely protective widowed mother who thought they weren't good enough for her daughter and had no qualms about telling them so. But when Jean had begged, 'Not this one Mum, please. This one's special,' she had scowled but promised not to criticise. In the event, the promise had been unnecessary. Muriel had adored Brian from the minute she met him, and he had become very fond of her.

Jean felt more cheerful as she reminded herself that she wouldn't be taking her mother off on holiday alone. Brian would be there to help.

Muriel's voice floated through from the kitchen, edged with the beginning of panic.

'Jean. Where are you, Jean?'

'In here, Mum. What's the problem?'

Muriel appeared at the door, her face full of puzzlement.

'I can't find the teapot anywhere.'

'It's here on the table, Mum. I'll bring it out for you.'

She took the teapot and the two mugs out into the kitchen,

and poured away the tea Muriel had made earlier. She reached out her hand to feel the kettle; it was cold. She switched it on, then put an arm round Muriel's shoulders.

'Come back into the living room, Mum, while we wait for the kettle to boil. I've got something to show you.'

Back at the table, she opened the brochure at the photograph of the hotel, set into the side of spectacular cliffs overlooking the harbour.

'You'll like it there, Mum. You went there before, years ago. On your honeymoon. Do you remember? You always said it was the most beautiful place you'd ever seen, and you'd love to go back one day.'

Muriel peered at the photograph with no sign of recognition.

'Lovely, dear,' she murmured vaguely, 'Now, how about a nice pot of tea? I'll put the kettle on, shall I?' and she wandered back out into the kitchen.

When she came back in with the teapot and two mugs on a tray, Jean tried again.

'This is where we're going on holiday, Mum. You went there before, once. But it was a long time ago. I don't expect you still remember the place. Come and sit here, and look through the brochure with me.'

Muriel set the tray carefully on the table, and frowned down at her daughter.

'I do wish you wouldn't talk to me as if I'm still in Infant School. Of course I remember Longuey perfectly. Why on earth shouldn't I? Beautiful island. Your father and I spent our honeymoon there, you know.'

With perfect confidence, she lifted the teapot and began to pour.

Jean didn't know whether to laugh or cry as she watched

the clear stream of hot water descending into the unwashed mugs.

* * *

The agency nurse bent over the old man's sleeping figure and gently lifted his wrist to feel for the pulse. As she counted the strong, steady beats, she noted his breathing, shallow but regular, and the colour in his cheeks. Nothing much wrong with this patient physically, apart from severe arthritis and failing eyesight. He was recovering well from his hip replacement operation, his heart was as sound as a bell, and he'd probably go on for a good many years yet.

The remaining problems were all rooted inside his head: the nightmares and panic attacks that left him sobbing and helpless, and the strange, almost catatonic states of withdrawal that sometimes overwhelmed him in the day. She didn't altogether approve of the attitude of the son and daughter-in-law. All the old man really needed now was large doses of tender loving care, and they should be providing it, not paying a nurse to do it for them. But the pay was good, and the nursing not too heavy, so she wasn't going to grumble. In any case, the job was coming to an end soon; she wasn't really needed any more here, whatever the daughter-in-law said.

She picked up the holiday brochure that had slipped from his fingers on to the floor, and straightened the armchair cushions to make him more comfortable. He stirred and sighed and settled back into sleep, and she thought that she hadn't seen him so peacefully relaxed for some time. Perhaps this coming holiday in the Channel Islands would do him a lot of good.

* * *

'You can't do that!'

'Of course I can. Why ever shouldn't I?'

'It would be totally out of keeping with the rest of the island. Besides, you haven't got the capital.'

Bernard Martel opened his mouth to protest, but his wife Claire swept on,

'And anyway, I don't give my permission.'

'I don't need your permission.'

'Oh yes you do! The island lease may be in joint names, but the house and the cottage are mine. Not ours, Bernard, *mine*. Mum and Dad left them specifically to me. Dad never trusted your judgement; he didn't want you to be able to take over the house and ruin it.'

'That's not fair. He was happy enough with the way I built up the hotel business.'

'*We* built up the hotel.' corrected Claire.

'Yes, of course, that's what I meant. And we could still work together now, to develop this new scheme. Don't fight me like this, please, I need you. You know we've always worked well together as a team.'

'Because we agreed on the aims. But I don't think that's true any more. Now you've started to see Longuey as something to exploit rather than preserve.'

'Preserve!' sneered Bernard, 'Here we go again. You sound just like your parents. That's all your father ever wanted to do, wasn't it? Keep everything as it was at all costs. Fight modernisations every step of the way. If it hadn't been for me, he would have preserved the island all the way into bankruptcy.'

'How dare you speak about Dad like that!' snapped

Claire. 'He was a better man than you'll ever be, and you know it.'

Bernard saw that he'd gone too far. He forced himself to speak more gently.

'All right, I'm sorry. I shouldn't have said that. I know your parents had a tough time here after the war. But it's not been easy for me either, you must know that. I often felt, while they were still alive, that the three of you were ganging up on me – treating me as an outsider.'

'Don't be silly – that's ridiculous,' said Claire, 'You grew up in the islands too, didn't you? That's why ...' Her voice trailed off as she saw what she was about to say.

'That's why you chose me.' finished Bernard bitterly. 'Yes, that says it all, doesn't it. I often used to wonder, you know. Why me? How can I be this lucky? Well, I know now, don't I? You weren't looking for a husband at all – you were looking for a suitable Estate Manager!'

Claire flushed, but didn't reply. Bernard's taunt was a familiar one from previous quarrels. At first she'd tried to protest and bluster, but eventually she had to admit to herself that what he said was essentially true. It shouldn't have mattered, though. They'd built up a marriage as they'd built up the hotel, and she'd thought their relationship was secure.

Until this last year, when she'd begun to discover just how shaky the foundations actually were.

Annoyed by her silence, Bernard raised his voice as he went on,

'Well, an Estate Manager is exactly what you got. And manage is exactly what I intend to go on doing. It's what I'm good at. So I suggest, if you're not willing to help me, that you just get the hell out of my life and leave me to get on with things as I see fit. I'd prefer to do all this *with* you. But I'll develop this island to its maximum potential whether you support me or not, and you needn't think you can stop me!'

'We'll see about that!' said Claire, her voice low and controlled but the anger unmistakable. 'I think I *can* stop you, at any rate as far as the house and cottage are concerned. I can certainly make life very difficult for you. And with my name on the lease too, you can't simply go ahead and do exactly what you like with the rest of the island without consulting me. Just where do you think you're going to get the capital for all this, anyway?'

'Don't you worry about that. I've got contacts. There are plenty of people around with the sense to see what a great investment opportunity this place offers.'

'But what about me? What about Robbie? Don't we count for anything? Can't you see what all this is doing to him?'

Bernard's face softened.

'Robbie,' he said sadly, 'Yes, I'm sorry if Robbie's upset. But *you* were the one who decided to move out of the hotel and flounce off to the cottage, so it's hardly my fault if the boy's feeling torn between us, is it? You know you can move back any time you like.'

Claire shook her head.

'I need time to sort myself out – think things through. It's no good coming back and pretending everything's all right between us just for Robbie's benefit. He's much too sensitive to be fooled by that.'

'Take time, by all means. Think carefully. I'm sure you'll come to see that I'm right, and that it's best for the family in the end if we all pull together.'

Claire could contain her anger no longer.

'You pretentious, arrogant, self-opinionated bastard!' she shouted. 'I thought you were pompous the very first time I met you, and by God you haven't improved one little bit since!'

She swept out of Bernard's office, slamming the door behind her.

## CHAPTER 2

The rain pattered remorselessly on the tent above their heads. Robbie, who'd been camping before, knew enough to resist the temptation to reach out a hand and draw a finger down the inside of the canvas. There was already an ominous dark patch developing where Lovering had done exactly that, and soon it would begin to drip.

Robbie was regretting his decision to come on the school Scout camp, which always ran in the week immediately after the end of the Summer term. He'd enjoyed it when he was younger, but was beginning to feel he'd outgrown the whole idea of Scouts. This year the camp looked like being a complete washout – literally. The rain had begun on the first day, retreating into a miserable misty drizzle on the second, and returning with a vengeance today. Mr. Hoskins, who'd been running the camp for as long as anyone could remember, did his best to keep everybody's spirits up, but even he was beginning to look gloomy.

'Poor old Husky!' said Lovering. 'I think he's definitely flagging. Have you noticed, he's even stopped going on about a scout smiling and whistling under all difficulties?'

‘Thank God for that, anyway,’ said Robbie, ‘Whistling! I ask you, Hal, when did you last hear of anyone whistling?’

Robbie had first met Henry Alexander Lovering the day after seeing the film ‘2001 : A Space Odyssey’, and immediately christened him Hal, after the ship’s computer.

‘Whistling is gross,’ agreed Lovering. ‘Where does he get these stupid ideas, anyway?’

‘It’s from “Scouting for Boys”. Old Husky’s always quoting odd bits from that. Do you know, he’s actually got a copy of it. I’ve seen it. Belongs in an antiquarian bookshop.’

Lovering snorted.

‘Typical! Why did we ever get ourselves involved with a dinosaur like Husky? The man came out of the Ark. Hey – that means he ought to be well able to cope with a spot of rain. He’s in his element!’

There was no response from Robbie, who was leaning out of his sleeping bag to rummage in his rucksack, so Lovering prodded him.

‘In his element! Rain – water – element. Oh, I give up! What’s the use of working on being a wit if even your best mate doesn’t appreciate you?’

‘Half-wit, more like,’ said Robbie, ‘That was only half a joke. Unworthy of you, Hal; you can do better than that. Anyway, the first bit was mixed metaphors, wasn’t it? Dinosaurs and Noah.’

‘Oh, I don’t know. There could have been dinosaurs on the Ark. Two of each sort.’

Robbie produced a personal stereo from the depths of the rucksack and began to untangle the headphone lead.

‘Is that the Walkman you got from Henderson?’

‘Yes. It did only need new batteries, and it’s got a radio as well. Good old Henderson – he has his uses. I know he’s a prat, but he's not really an obnoxious prat. Well, not all of the time, anyway.'

Lovering considered this statement carefully.

'It depends what you mean by obnoxious,' he said, 'I can't say I warm to the precious Dominic, myself. His mother's obnoxious pretty much all of the time, and it's probably inherited. Do you think there's a dominant gene for obnoxiousness? Is that the right noun from obnoxious? Obnoxity, perhaps? Obnoction? How about obnoctation? Sort of combining obnoxious and ostentation. Now, that would do very nicely for Mrs. Henderson.'

'Do shut up wittering, Hal, and let me listen to the weather forecast.'

'Don't know what you want a weather forecast for,' muttered Lovering gloomily, 'I can tell you the weather. It's wet. And it's going to stay wet all week.'

'It might not,' said Robbie, 'Don't be such a pessimist, Hal.'

Lovering lapsed into silence while Robbie listened on the headphones. At the end of the weather bulletin, Robbie switched the radio off.

'O.K. You win. It's going to stay wet. Probably all week.'

Lovering grinned.

'That's the beauty of being a pessimist,' he said cheerfully, 'When things are bad, at least you get the pleasure of being proved right. Whereas poor old optimists like you, Robbie, always end up being disappointed.'

'It's not just disappointing, it's frustrating. There was a bit about 'high pressure centred over the extreme South'. That means while we're waterlogged here, it's probably glorious sunshine on Longuey, and set fair for the rest of the week. Mum said it was a lovely day there yesterday.'

'Was that when you went and phoned her from the village?' asked Lovering. 'I didn't see you when you came back, because I was on the cooking rota. How was your Mum?'

'Call that cooking? They should call it the poisoning rota.'

There was a long silence.

'O.K.' said Lovering at last, 'If you don't want to talk about it, that's fine. But I'm not stupid, you know, Robbie. I did notice you were upset about something yesterday. You went all quiet on me last night.'

In spite of his uncontrollable tendency towards banter and repartee, which was at least partly a defence mechanism against his own problems, Lovering was both perceptive and sensitive. Not for the first time, Robbie was thankful for a sympathetic hearer who would make no demands on him.

'Mum's moved out of the hotel,' he said flatly. His fingers mechanically wound and re-wound the lead of the Walkman, and he didn't look up at Lovering. 'I'm going to spend half the holiday with her in the cottage, and then go to the hotel with Dad. I think they've had another big row. She was trying hard not to sound upset yesterday, but she was.'

'That's rotten,' said Lovering quietly. He managed to make it a simple statement of fact, and Robbie was grateful. He was at the stage of distress where too kind a word would have sent him over the edge of self-control into tears, and he didn't want that. He did very much want to cry, but he knew exactly where he wanted to do it, and it wasn't here.

'It might actually be a bit better than it was at half term,' he said, when he was sure he could control the tremble in his voice. 'They can only row when they're together, can't they? So I won't have to listen to them shouting at each other. Or even worse, trying not to shout because they remember I'm there.'

Lovering nodded.

'I know. It'll still be rotten, though. You'll have to listen to each of them separately going on about the other one.'

He spoke with the voice of experience. His parents had split up the year before, and he'd only recently managed to establish a very uneasy truce with his new stepfather.

'I don't think mine will do that,' said Robbie. 'At least, I suppose Mum might, a bit. But Dad will just not mention it at all, and try to pretend everything's normal.'

'Like you, you mean?' asked Lovering shrewdly.

Robbie had never thought about it before, but he saw that it was true.

'Yes,' he said, 'Dad and I are very alike, really. That's why I understand so well how he feels. But the awful thing is, Hal, that I nearly always know it's Mum who's right.'

'You can't take sides,' said Lovering firmly. 'I don't really know much about anything, but I do know that. You've got to stay out of it, if you can, and let them sort it out for themselves. It's the only way.'

'I know,' said Robbie. 'It's just not easy. I wish you were coming to stay this year, Hal.'

'So do I. But Mum wants me around at home this summer – to get to know Peter better, she says. Oh God, Robbie – he wants to take me fishing!'

It was Robbie's turn to sympathise. He knew how much Hal had loved going fishing with his father.

'We can still write to each other,' he said, trying to sound cheerful. 'And phone. Don't let the buggers get you down, Hal.'

'Oh, I don't think the phones are bugged!' said Lovering, reverting to banter, and Robbie threw a pillow at him.

There were heavily squelchy footsteps outside the tent.

'Now then, you two, settle down. I'll just slacken off your

guy lines for you, in case it goes on raining all night. See you bright and early on the breakfast rota, Martel.'

'Yes, Mr Hoskins,' said Robbie meekly.

'Goodnight then, lads.'

'Night, Sir.'

The footsteps sploshed away, followed by a prolonged slithering sound, a heavy thud, and muffled curses. The boys subsided into helpless giggles, then settled deeper into their sleeping bags and fell silent. Soon Lovering was snoring gently. Robbie lay awake listening to the rain, and thinking of Longuey. It was his mother he'd spoken to most recently, and who would meet him when he arrived back on the island. But it was his father, and the hotel, he found himself thinking of as he finally drifted off into sleep.

* * *

In the dining room of the Dolphin Hotel, Bernard Martel was making his usual social round at the end of dinner, paying particular attention to the newcomers. He bent solicitously over the table of two elderly spinsters who had arrived on the afternoon ferry.

'Good evening, ladies. Good to see you back with us again. I hope you had a pleasant journey?'

'Oh yes, thank you Bernard. Our flight to Guernsey was right on time, and the ferry trip was a pleasure, the sea was so calm. Not like last year, when it was almost too rough to land, do you remember?'

Her companion nodded vigorously and joined in,

'I don't think we'd ever been so wet. When we finally made it up to the hotel, Claire made us hot toddies – at three in the afternoon!' She looked vaguely round the dining room.

'We haven't seen anything of Claire this evening, Bernard. I do hope she's not unwell?'

'No, no – just very busy. She's extending the range of goods in the craft shop this year, so she's having to spend a lot of her time in the pottery. And she goes across to France quite often, so you may not see much of her at all this year.'

'Oh, poor Bernard. You must miss her about the hotel. Such a lovely girl. And so popular with all the guests.'

'Yes,' murmured Bernard, his smile fixed. 'Now if you'll just excuse me, ladies ...'

He drifted away towards the next table, where Neville Blythe was deep in conversation with a stunningly beautiful dark-haired girl in a dress the colour of Beaujolais. Neville looked up briefly and caught Bernard's eye.

'Ah, Bernard. Ten o'clock tomorrow morning. Your office. All right?'

It was not really a question. Neville had turned back to the girl even before Bernard nodded in acquiescence.

'Fine, Neville. No problem.'

There *was* a problem, because there was a party of businessmen arriving on the ten o'clock ferry and Bernard should be there to meet them, but it was no use saying so. He'd just have to arrange for someone else to be there to welcome them.

He moved on to chat briefly with Brian Wilson, who sat alone at his family's table, still lingering over coffee. Bernard had noticed earlier that Muriel had not come down to join the Wilsons for dinner, and Jean had left the dining room early, presumably to help her mother to bed. He enquired politely after the old lady's health; Brian assured him that Muriel had simply stayed out in the sun a little too long, and decided on an early night.

Bernard murmured words of sympathy, and continued

on his round of the dining room. This was one of the parts of his job that he was actually rather good at, though he didn't particularly enjoy it. He smoothly placated the brash American couple at the next table, who had complained about their soup and sent it back, bringing their waitress close to tears. He managed to laugh convincingly at the ponderous jokes of the portly, red-faced Yorkshire businessman with the mousy, downtrodden wife. He retreated tactfully, with no more than a brief 'Good evening', from the French publisher who was leaning across the table to gaze intently into his companion's eyes. Then he headed purposefully towards the Taylor family's table, in the best position by the window with a spectacular view down over the harbour and the bay beyond.

Paul Taylor was an impressive figure, with his silver-grey hair and startlingly blue eyes. He still retained an air of quiet authority, in spite of the stresses of recent illness and encroaching age. Bernard didn't envy Paul's son, Richard. Taking over such a huge company on his father's retirement couldn't have been easy, however much he'd been groomed for the job beforehand. Sarah, Richard's wife, smiled easily at Bernard as he approached their table.

'Hello, Bernard. Can you come and join us, or are you too busy?'

'Everything under control for the moment, Sarah. I think I can afford to give myself some time off.'

He drew up a chair from the next table and sat beside her. It was amazing how quickly she'd swung into the easy familiarity with which she now treated him. There were families who had been coming to stay at the hotel for years and who still hardly spoke to him. Sarah and Richard had come to the island for the first time last year, and within hours Sarah had insisted on treating Bernard and Claire like old friends, much to Richard's initial embarrassment. But Bernard was grateful, because the relationship struck up so artificially by Sarah had led to an understanding with Richard that could prove very fruitful. He had wondered what complications to expect from the presence this year of Richard's father, but the old man seemed tired and preoccupied for much of the time, and Richard never seemed to discuss business with him.

'I hope you enjoyed your meal?'

'Yes, of course, Bernard. Quite up to your usual high standards.'

Bernard smiled ruefully.

'I'm glad you think so!'

Sarah leaned forward and patted his hand.

'That American is a quite dreadful woman. She does nothing but grumble the whole time. I thought you dealt with her beautifully, Bernard. I would have wrung her neck.'

'They're leaving tomorrow morning,' said Bernard thankfully, 'It's just as well. Another week and I would wring the wretched woman's neck.'

Richard laughed.

'Not a good idea, Bernard. I know they say any publicity is good publicity, but murdering one of the guests would be going a bit too far! Articles in the quality Sunday supplements, that's what we want, not the tabloids camped on the beaches.'

Bernard noted the intensity of Paul's glance at Richard, and wondered if he'd picked up the use of the word 'we'. He wasn't sure how much Richard had told his father about their plans, or whether the old man would approve. He was saved from an obvious attempt to change the subject by Sarah's intervention.

'Well, I think the soup was wonderful. What do

Americans know about good food anyway, especially French cuisine? You're so lucky to have kept Jean-Pierre as your chef, Bernard. I would have thought he might be tempted by the offer he had last year from that big hotel in Jersey.'

Bernard settled thankfully into the safer topic of general domestic and culinary details. There would be time enough to talk to Richard about publicity tomorrow.

# CHAPTER 3

Robbie was right – the weather on Longuey was sunny all week and looked as if it might continue into a second. By mid-morning on Monday the sun was already hot enough to burn through the first layer of suntan lotion. The more sensible and well-prepared day-trippers wore floppy sunhats, and struggled off the ferry laden with beach umbrellas as well as rush mats, canvas chairs and cool-boxes.

They came in groups, in families, in pairs, alone; scrambling from the ferry and up the harbour steps to disperse and go their different ways. Some stayed close to the harbour, browsing in the gift shops, settling in the lounge bar of the pub or spreading themselves out on the nearest stretch of sand. Others headed along the various paths to beaches, sand-dunes or cliffs. A few struggled up the steep path to the hotel.

The temperature rose steadily. The main beaches attracted the majority of the day-trippers, clustering thickly round the sources of refreshment like iron filings round a magnet. Further out from the epicentres of ice-cream dependency, there was plenty of room for those seeking more solitude.

Pockets of sand within the dunes provided refuges completely cut off from one another, except for snatches of sound drifting on the still air.

'You put that down *at once,* Darren! Do you hear me?'

'Anyone fancy another swim before lunch? Race you out to the big rock and back.'

'I know that face!'

'Hold it just like that for a minute while I change the lens, love. No, don't move. Oh no – what did you want to move for? That would have been a brilliant shot if only you'd waited for me to get the exposure right.'

'Darren! I'm not telling you again – you leave our Sandra alone!'

'If you're going to the kiosk, get us a cheese and pickle sandwich and a packet of salt and vinegar crisps, there's a dear.'

'God! Sodding sand! All these sharp little bits of shell, they stick to your skin like bloody Araldite. Give me Torremolinos any day!'

'I'm *positive* I remember that face from somewhere.'

'Don't be a cry-baby, Darren. I'm sure Sandra didn't mean it.'

* * *

In the hotel, Bernard had already had a second meeting with Neville and was now deep in discussions with Richard. Sarah took her father-in-law to his room. She offered to stay and play Scrabble with him until lunch, but the heat was making him restless and he refused, rather tetchily. She saw the danger signs and retreated, first settling him into a chair out on his balcony. Downstairs in the lounge she stood for a while running a finger half-heartedly along the row of books on the bookshelf, then went to join Jean Wilson, who was sitting at a low table by the window sorting out the edge pieces of a jigsaw.

The sun crept higher in the sky, the old man dozed fitfully on his balcony, and the sounds of their voices drifted out of the open windows of the lounge, to mingle with the clatter of lunch preparations in the kitchen.

'She's quite lucid some of the time, you see. In a way, that makes it worse.'

'Oh my dear, I know just what you mean. I went through exactly the same thing with my own mother. And now we're beginning to have very similar problems with Richard's father. I don't think he's ever really been the same since he had to give up running the business.'

'With Mum, it's only really got bad in the last year or so. But I think she's getting worse quite quickly now. I really don't know how I'd cope if it wasn't for Brian. He's marvellous with her – he's taken her off to the beach this morning, to give me a break.'

'You're lucky to have him. It must be a great comfort.'

'Oh yes, it is. It's amazing really what you can put up with, if you just feel you have someone to support you.'

'I wish I could feel like that about Richard. His first priority is always the business. He let me struggle on with my mother until she died, and never gave me any help or support at all. I thought it might be different now that it's his own father. But the trouble with him is he never even wants to admit there's any problem.'

* * *

Further along the ground floor, the windows of Bernard's office were also wide open.

‘I don’t foresee any problems, Richard. This should be a straightforward business deal, with a high return for minimum risk. Ideally, we want to keep the consortium small, just the three of us, which is why the initial investment demanded is high. But if you can’t manage all of that amount, I’m sure Neville and I could find a fourth to come in on the scheme, to relieve you of some of the financial pressure. Some of the profit too, of course.’

‘No, no, Bernard. That won’t be necessary. I can find the capital all right. I was thinking more in terms of problems at your end. What about the terms of the lease?’

‘You leave the lease to me. It will all be taken care of. What we have to worry about now is publicity.’

‘Really? I would have thought you already had a good publicity set-up for the hotel. Surely it will be easy enough to extend that to cover the new developments?’

‘You misunderstand me, Richard. I mean we have to worry about ensuring a *lack* of publicity at this stage.’

* * *

On the longest Westward-facing beach, lunchtime came and went; the sun began its slow slide down the sky, and the tide steadily receded as if aiming to meet it on the horizon. Dedicated sun-worshippers changed the position of their towels and mats, to catch the magical rays at the optimum angle.

The level of activity on the beach decreased as the processes of digestion continued, in many cases to be followed by sleep. Beached whales of both sexes slumbered under the pages of paperbacks; babies crumpled sideways under the canopies of pushchairs; a toddler in a sunhat, his mouth smeared with dried ice-cream and traces of sand, staggered on the uneven sand like a miniature Oliver Reed, sat down with a sudden bump and toppled gently into an instant doze.

The tide withdrew steadily, exposing a maze of rock pools. The shallow slope of the beach allowed paddlers to explore a long way out and still be only up to their knees in water, so children played safely while their parents relaxed into lazy inactivity. Even the groups of teenagers seemed muted, their movements slowed to the steady trudge across the sand for ice-creams, or the peculiarly awkward gait of the barefoot journey across sharp shingle below the high tide mark.

Sounds still carried in the breezeless air, but the thick heat of the afternoon muffled and absorbed them: a herring-gull screeching as it harassed a smaller gull with food in its beak; the drone of a plane high overhead; voices on the path behind the dunes.

'It's going ahead, and you can't stop it.'

'Over my dead body!'

The larger gull screamed in triumph and swooped on the crust of bread the smaller bird dropped.

* * *

The end of the afternoon brought the first faint wisps of cloud to the sky. By the time the day-trippers were gathering their belongings to head for the last ferry back to Guernsey, the streaks of white had run together into broad strips of cloud, some of them deepening to grey. The sun continued to sink gently through the layers. Occasionally it stabbed through the gaps, giving a final polish to reddened shoulders and backs of knees that would only start to hurt later in the evening.

The students manning the kiosks began their clearing up

as the exodus from the beaches continued. The steady stream of figures wound back along the paths to the harbour; some happier, some crosser, all hotter than when they had arrived.

Bernard was there to meet the ferry as it docked, greeting the new arrivals for the hotel and organising their luggage into the trailer that would take it up the steep cliff-side drive for them. He busied himself in conversation with the first couple off the boat, and bustled them off up the path, not looking back at the one large and rather battered suitcase he had left standing alone by the harbour wall.

Claire stepped forward to pick up the suitcase, and greeted the last passenger off the ferry.

'Hello, Mum,' said Robbie.

# CHAPTER 4

After a week of glorious sunshine, Robbie's first full day on Longuey dawned grey and threatening. The night before, he'd thumped his head five times on the pillow before he went to sleep, in the ritual his mother had taught him for waking on time without an alarm clock. It never seemed to work at school, only here on the island, the magic reinforced by the excitement of holidays. Minutes after he opened his eyes, he heard the bleeping of his watch from the bedside table; magic was magic, but bets could always be hedged. On the first morning on the island, it was a point of honour to be in the sea before six, and it was a long walk from the cottage to the best bay for swimming.

He knew even before he pulled the edge of the curtain aside to look out that the weather had changed. The light that already seeped through the curtains was heavy and sluggish and not at all inviting. But a point of honour shouldn't be sacrificed for the sake of a few clouds, however glowering, and at least it wasn't yet raining. He pulled on his clothes over swimming trunks, took his towel in a carrier bag, and let himself out, closing the front door carefully behind him so as not to disturb his mother.

Halfway up the long hill behind the cottage the rain began; a light drizzle that settled in a film on his hair and eventually began trickling down the side of his nose. His jacket was reasonably waterproof, but he wished he'd worn the one that had a hood. When he came out on to the cliff path at the top, the wind whipped the tiny droplets more viciously into his face, and he blinked as he looked out over a sea breaking up into peaklets of foam like a carelessly iced cake. He was glad when at last he reached the steep steps leading down to the comparative shelter of the bay. He slowed down to negotiate the first few, partly because the rain had made them slippery, but mainly to postpone his arrival at the point where the steps rounded a corner and the whole of the bay became visible. He always savoured this moment at the beginning of the holiday when he first saw the empty beach spread out in the early morning just for him.

The disappointment hit him like a blow. He was not the only early visitor to the beach; not even the only swimmer. He felt a quite unreasonable fury at the sight of the pile of clothes and the towel, spread out on a rock just above the high water mark, and the dark head that bobbed gently in the water quite a long way out.

Wrapped up in his indignation at this violation of what he regarded as his own private beach, he took a long time to register the significance of two facts. The tide was more than halfway out, and the single line of footprints leading out across the wet sand finished a long way short of the edge of the water. And the head was dark because it remained face-downwards, moving gently only as the waves caught it.

* * *

Robbie stood transfixed, his eyes staring out at the figure in the water while thoughts tumbled over one another inside his head. Perhaps it was someone snorkelling; but no – there was no sign of a tube above the surface, and no forward movement through the water. This was a body. No, perhaps not yet a body; perhaps a swimmer in difficulties who could be rescued. Surely a drowned body wouldn't still be floating? Should he try to swim out? It was a long way out, where the water was deep and the current beginning to be treacherous, and he knew he wasn't a strong enough swimmer to bring someone back that far. He had done lifesaving at school, but that was with another boy, in a swimming pool, and he'd only just managed it; in the open sea with what looked like an adult he wouldn't have much of a chance. No sense ending up with two people drowned.

Even as his mind made the decision and knew that it was the sensible one, his body followed different instincts, and he stumbled down the rest of the steps on to the beach and began to run towards the edge of the water. As he ran he shouted, hoping against all reason for a response.

Before he reached the water he stopped. There was no reply to his shouting. The dark head bobbed with the waves, grotesquely nodding at him as the swell caught it. From the level of the beach he could see more clearly that the face was completely submerged. He wondered again why the body should be floating; then remembered the line of lobster pots that looped out from the rocks at the edge of this bay. The body must somehow be caught up with one of the floats that marked their positions.

Still he hesitated, his eyes straining to see what he knew couldn't be possible; a movement of limbs or head not caused by the rolling of the water. It was only when he turned away and looked at the line of footprints that he was fully convinced. The gap between the end of the footprints and the beginning of the water spoke of hours, not minutes, since the swimmer had entered the sea. In some ways the knowledge was a relief. His responsibility now was to report a fatality, not to try to save a life. But the realisation of his closeness to a death brought a faint queasiness, and the beginnings of a tremble in his legs. To quell both, he concentrated on ordering his thoughts, and found himself muttering aloud.

'What to do first? No sense trying to swim out. It'll take more than one person – probably a boat. It will have to be reported to the mainland, I suppose, and they'll send someone to investigate. I wish I had a camera. If the weather gets any worse, the rain might wash out the footprints. The clothes will get soaked, too. Wonder if I ought to move them? Better not, perhaps. Get help as soon as possible, that's the thing. Now the tide's coming in again, the footprints will get wiped out anyway. And if the wind gets up any more, the body may well shift and sink. I ought to try to fix its position, in case it's not there when I bring people back.'

He rubbed the rain from his eyes and stared out across the water.

'Right – fourth float out from this end. About level with that outcrop at the top of the cliff.'

He turned and started back towards the steps. Above the high water mark the sand had already acquired a wet crust from the rain, and his canvas shoes crunched through it to the drier sand beneath. A sudden thought struck him, and he went back to the rock where the pile of clothes lay. Taking his own towel out of the plastic carrier he'd brought it in, he pulled at the corner of the bag with his teeth until it split. When he tore carefully down the side and along the bottom, the opened out rectangle was big enough to cover the neatly folded pile of clothes, though not the towel spread out beside them. He tucked two corners of the plastic under the edge of the towel and weighed down the other two with pebbles.

'There – best I can do. I've not really disturbed anything, and now they won't get completely sodden. Pity about the towel, but I don't suppose that matters.'

He stood for a moment frowning down at his handiwork. Something was niggling at him; something was odd, but he couldn't for the life of him think what it was.

A sudden gust of wind blew rain into his face, and he was reminded of the urgency of the situation – the weather *was* definitely worsening. He stuffed his own towel inside his jacket and hurried to the steps. At the corner halfway up he stopped and glanced back down at the water. The waves were higher, tugging more insistently at the body, but it was still there. The bay would stay sheltered from the worst of the weather unless the wind changed direction. At the top of the cliff he gasped as the wind hit him, put his head down to stop the rain lashing into his eyes, and ran along the cliff path.

The effort of running, concentrating on his breathing and looking down at his feet, prevented him from thinking. It was only when he stopped to catch his breath and wipe the rain from his face that he faced his next decision.

'Which way? Hotel or cottage?'

The path forked at the top of the hill leading down to the cottage, and if he branched off to the left he could get straight across to the back entrance to the hotel grounds. He knew the hotel was the sensible place to aim for; if he went down to the cottage first he would probably waste valuable time climbing back up to the level of the hotel to find his father and some of the other staff. But he knew that it was his mother he needed to see; he must tell her before he could face telling anyone else. As he ran down the hill, he told himself it was a rational choice after all. He could phone the hotel from the cottage, and they could meet him back at the top of the hill, so no time would be wasted. Part of his mind was convinced by the justification, but he knew really that the need for his mother was both irrational and completely overwhelming.

By the time he stumbled through the front door he was panting with exhaustion and the shock was beginning to hit him hard. He stood trembling in the living room, water streaming off him onto the carpet, and howled like the little boy he suddenly felt.

'Mum!'

There was no reply.

It was some time before he gathered his senses together and made the effort to move and go to look for her.

The cottage was empty. His mother's bedroom was deserted; the bed neatly made with no clue to whether it had been slept in or not. She wasn't there.

* * *

At the hotel there were already signs of life. The chef Jean-Pierre was pouring himself the first cup of strong black French coffee in the kitchen; the cleaning staff had arrived to work on the lounge and dining room; Bernard had unlocked the front door and opened up his office. Most of the guests were still soundly asleep, but in some rooms there was movement.

Neville Blythe slept like a child, his face relaxed and peaceful and his breathing steady. His hand flung out on the pillow beside him filled an empty space; the other side of the bed was unoccupied, and from the bathroom came the noise of the shower. When it stopped, Abigail came out swathed in towels. She sat in front of the mirror and reached for the hairdryer, then changed her mind and prowled restlessly round the room, rubbing vigorously at her hair with the small towel that had been wound round it. Neville stirred, turned over, and reached out a lazy hand to catch at her wrist as she passed.

'Take that stupid towel off and come back to bed!'

'For Christ's sake, Neville – not now! Leave me alone; I want to think.'

Further along the corridor, Sarah sat at Paul's bedside. The old man tossed and turned and mumbled in his sleep, and she held his hand and stroked it mechanically. Earlier, when he had sat bolt upright, his eyes staring and his limbs thrashing, she had held him more tightly in her arms until the worst was over and he sank back into exhaustion. Now his breathing was gradually deepening, and the muttering only occasionally formed itself into distinguishable words.

'Dead. Dead. Doesn't matter. All dead now.'

Outside the main hotel building, in the separate block of self-contained rooms, the French publisher snored loudly, hearing nothing of the movements of his companion.

In the kitchen, Jean-Pierre looked up from his coffee in surprise as Muriel, her hair in curlers and her dressing gown flapping open where the belt was coming untied, wandered in and beamed at him.

'Bonjour, Jean-Pierre!' she said brightly, in a faultless accent, and wandered out again.

In the office, Bernard was sitting right beside the telephone, and when it rang he picked it up almost immediately. He listened for a while, then broke in on the incoherent babble coming from the other end.

'Robbie! Just stop for a minute and calm down. Take a deep breath, try not to panic, and tell me again. Slowly!'

He listened, frowning in concentration.

'O.K. Robbie. Don't worry. You did all the right things.

You can leave it to me now. I'll organise some of the staff and we'll get a boat round there. You'd better stay where you are, in case your mother comes back.'

His frown deepened as he listened to Robbie's reply.

'All right, then, if you must. I'm not sure that it's a good idea, but I can't really stop you if you're sure you want to come. I'll meet you at the top of the path.'

In the cottage, Robbie put the phone down with a sigh of relief. He *didn't* particularly want to go back to that dreadful bobbing figure. But he wanted to be alone even less.

# CHAPTER 5

Robbie's first instinct was to leave the cottage immediately, but he hesitated at the door and thought again. It would take his father a while to find help, and organise the boat. He might as well use some of that time to get himself better protected against the weather. He stripped off his sodden coat and found his cagoule, then rummaged in the hall cupboard for his wellingtons. When he opened the door and went out he was glad of the cagoule's hood. The rain was coming down heavily now, and had clearly settled in for the day. He trudged up the hill, not bothering to look ahead through the driving rain, but concentrating on his feet. He wasn't expecting to meet anyone until he reached the top, so he let out a startled yelp when he heard his name and looked up to see the figure that he had nearly walked straight into.

'Robbie! You're surely not going swimming in this weather?'

His mother was on her way down the hill, her shoulders hunched against the rain and her wet hair clinging to her face. Robbie startled her by flinging his arms around her and hugging her tightly; then he let her go and found himself shouting through the rain into her face.

'Where were you? I couldn't find you anywhere. Where the hell have you been?'

'I was at the pottery. I couldn't sleep, so I got up really early and went to finish off some pots. For heaven's sake, Robbie, what's got into you? Why are you so upset about it?'

'You weren't there!' he shouted, 'I needed you, Mum, and you weren't bloody there!'

She held his shoulders and looked into his face.

'Tell me!' she said. 'Calm down and tell me what's happened.'

He took her hand and dragged her on up the hill; she went with him in silence, and as they went he told her.

* * *

At the top of the hill they waited together at the fork in the path until they saw Bernard and Jean-Pierre coming to meet them. Bernard showed no sign of surprise at seeing Claire, but avoided her eyes and addressed himself to Robbie,

'You found her, then. Better get a move on, if you're coming. The boat should be there almost as soon as we are.'

He pushed on ahead of them at a brisk walk, not looking back to see if they were following.

When they reached the bay there was no sign of the boat. Robbie saw with relief that the dark shape in the water was still in the same position as before. Although the rain was heavier now, the wind was no stronger, and the insistent tugging of the waves hadn't managed to dislodge the body. It must be held fast, tangled in the line from the floats. He wondered now why he'd insisted on coming; there was nothing they could do from the beach. The boat when it came would probably haul the body aboard and then take it back around the coastline, without coming ashore here at all. He should have taken his mother back to the cottage, and left his father to take over.

Even as he thought it, he knew he couldn't really have done that. This was *his* beach, and his discovery. He had to be in on whatever happened next, even if it turned out to be unpleasant.

Bernard had brought a camera with him, and began by taking a couple of shots of the whole bay. Then he took several of the line of footprints, finishing with a close-up. Only then did he walk forward to the edge of the water, adding a third set of footprints to the ones already there; the double row out and back left by Robbie, and the single row outwards presumably made by the man in the water.

Jean-Pierre went to join Bernard, and they waved at the boat as it appeared round the headland and headed in to the bay. The men on the boat signalled back immediately; they hardly needed the pointing figures from the beach to direct them to the position of the body. Robbie thought they would probably have seen it as soon as they came round the corner into relatively calm water. There was quite a swell developing further out, but here it was still sheltered from the worst of the wind. It was just as well – they would have enough trouble as it was, keeping the boat steady close to the rocks as they freed the body from the lines and hauled it aboard.

Bernard came back to join Robbie and Claire at the high water mark.

'Where are the clothes you say you found, Rob?'

Robbie showed him, and Bernard stood looking down at the sodden towel.

'That's a hotel towel, almost certainly. I suppose he has to be one of the guests.'

'What shall we do with the clothes, Dad? I thought I'd better not move anything, but they were getting drenched.'

'You did the right thing. There will have to be some sort of investigation from the mainland; I'll phone the police from the office when we get back to the hotel, and they'll send someone over on the ferry. I expect they'll want things disturbed as little as possible.'

'Does that mean we have to try to keep people away?'

'Well, there won't be many people heading for the beaches in this weather anyway, but yes, I suppose we'll have to cordon off this bay altogether. We can't have any more feet trampling over it until the police have seen it.'

Out in the boat, two of the men were leaning over the side and struggling with the figure in the water, one supporting it while the other tried to disentangle the line. The head was out of the water now, and Robbie was glad it was too far away to be able to see clearly from the shore. He'd never actually seen a drowned body before, but he'd spent enough time with fishermen, both here and on Guernsey, to know what to expect. He'd heard the stories of faces nibbled by crabs and fish within hours of a body going into the water. He thought that was mainly true of bodies that sank to the bottom, but he had no wish to find out at first hand whether it applied to floating ones as well.

Claire was looking at the pile of clothes under its makeshift cover.

'Accident, do you think? Or could it be suicide? That's one of the first things you think of, isn't it? The classic situation; a pile of clothes left on a beach.'

'Accident,' said Robbie promptly.

'What makes you so definite?' asked Claire, surprised.

'The towel,' Robbie said. 'If you're going to commit

suicide by swimming out to sea, you're not going to take a towel with you to dry yourself off afterwards, are you?'

'I suppose not,' said Claire doubtfully, 'but I don't know – suicides do some pretty strange things. I'm not sure that you'd be thinking very logically if you were desperate enough to be thinking of killing yourself.'

Both men in the boat were leaning well over now, trying to get a good grip. There was a brief flurry of movement, then the dark figure was lifted from the water and rolled over the side. The men signalled again towards the shore, and Bernard waved in acknowledgement. Robbie watched as the boat swung round and headed back out of the bay.

'Where will they take it?' he asked, suddenly struck by a dreadful vision of a dripping body carried through the hotel as the guests were coming down for breakfast. 'Not the hotel, surely?'

Claire had clearly had much the same thought as Robbie. Bernard looked worried.

'Not initially, no – I told them to go to the old boathouse in the little bay beyond the harbour. But I'll have to decide what to do later; I'm not sure that we can keep the body there. It will have to do, though, until I've got through to the police in Guernsey to ask for advice.'

The boat had disappeared round the headland, and Jean-Pierre was already making his way back up the beach towards the steps, but Bernard hesitated.

'Do you think you ought to take a look at the clothes?' asked Robbie, 'If they belong to someone from the hotel, you might recognise them.'

'I suppose so,' said his father. Robbie gently loosened the edge of the plastic carrier and lifted it.

'Yes,' said Bernard, his voice flat and expressionless. 'Yes,

I know that shirt. The logo on the pocket's very distinctive. I've seen it before.'

Claire moved forward so that she could see, and Robbie heard her catch her breath.

'So have I,' she said. 'Oh God, Bernard, it must be Richard!'

# CHAPTER 6

That evening Robbie sat in his bedroom nursing a mug of hot chocolate, and tried to marshal his thoughts to set them down on paper in some kind of logical order.

*Dear Hal,* he wrote, *You won't believe this, but I've spent most of this afternoon being interviewed by a policeman! Well, all right — slight exaggeration. It wasn't quite all afternoon, and he did interview quite a few other people as well. But I really was the star witness, because I found the body!! (Pause while you pick yourself up off the floor, dust yourself down, and gasp, 'What body?')*

*There was a drowned body floating in our swimming bay this morning — the one where we went skinny-dipping at midnight last year, do you remember? Anyway, I went for my early swim, and there it was, so I get the credit for having discovered it. It wasn't very pleasant, actually — in fact it was rather horrible,* because it turned out to be someone we know. You might remember him, come to think of it – I'm pretty sure they were staying here while you were with us last year; Richard and Claire Taylor, the couple who won the treasure hunt and made us drink some of their champagne to celebrate. I didn't really like them much, to be honest – too pushy, and I always thought there was something odd about the way they latched on to Dad so quickly. But not liking someone doesn't stop you feeling a bit sick when you realise they're dead. It was him: Richard – the body, I mean. Dad recognised the clothes he'd been wearing – they were left in a pile on the beach – but his wife still had to go and identify him. I saw her immediately afterwards, and she looked really weird; all pale and icy, with eyes that looked right through you without seeing anything at all. Shock, I suppose.

That was bad enough, but it was even worse when they told the old man. Their father came with them this year, and he's not been well. When they told him Richard was dead, he went completely to pieces. Everyone in the hotel could hear him, sobbing like a baby, and sometimes letting out great howls of pain. It was awful. Like having to listen to someone being tortured.

Mum and Dad have been going frantic, trying to sort everything out without disrupting the hotel routine too much or frightening off any of the other guests. (At least they're actually speaking to each other – nothing like a spot of adversity to make warring factions close ranks.)

*I must say, the two policemen who came over on the ferry with the doctor have been very discreet. I think Dad was worried that they'd come barging in making themselves obvious all over the place, but they weren't like that at all. There was a constable in uniform, but we often have visiting constables on duty in the summer, so nobody took particular notice of him. The one with him was a plain-clothes sergeant, and very good at fading into the background – I think most of the people who came across him in the hotel just thought he was one of the guests.*

*Just think, Hal – I've now been interviewed by a real live S.O.C.O! Not that there is a scene of crime for him to be officer of, exactly, because it's just an accidental death, not a crime at all.*

Robbie stopped writing and sucked thoughtfully on the end of his pen, remembering the Sergeant's shrewd grey eyes, and his soft voice gently probing.

'What made you so sure it was a body, not just a swimmer?'

'The footprints.'

'Ah, yes – the footprints. Tell me about the footprints.'

'But I've told you already. And you've seen them for yourself. You went to the beach and photographed everything this morning.'

'I know, but tell me again, just the same. You saw them before the rain blurred them, and you saw them at a different state of the tide.'

'It was the gap; the gap between the end of the footprints and the edge of the sea. The tide must have been going out for hours since he went into the water. Nobody stays in swimming for that long. Especially at night.'

He'd not thought it out so clearly at the time; it had been more by instinct than conscious thought that he'd decided the body must be dead. In Bernard's office, facing the Sergeant's gentle but insistent questions, the reasoning became more distinct in his mind.

'About how long, would you say?'

'I'm not an expert on tides.'

'Never mind. You're a local; you know these beaches. An educated guess.'

'To go out from the point where the footprints stopped to where the tide was when I got there? Four hours – perhaps five, I don't know. But that makes it a bit odd, doesn't it?'

'Go on.'

'Well, that would make it about one or two in the morning when he went in. Funny time to go swimming.'

The Sergeant lifted one eyebrow and smiled at him.

'Funnier than six in the morning? In the rain?'

Robbie smiled back.

'But I always do that. I swim early most mornings, and always on the first day of the holiday. But I don't think Mr Taylor went swimming much at all – or not when he was here last year, anyway.'

'All right – let's go back to the clothes. You didn't move them at all?'

'No. Just covered them up to stop them getting soaked.'

'You didn't recognise the shirt, as your father did?'

'No, but I wouldn't, would I? I've only just arrived on the island, and I'm not staying in the hotel, so I'd not seen anybody much yet, except Mum. Mr Taylor wasn't the sort of person to wear anything this season that I'd recognise from last year.'

‘What about the towel?’

‘I didn’t notice it was a hotel one, if that’s what you mean. It was just a towel. Something someone had taken to go swimming with. There was this pile of clothes, and the towel, and someone in the water. It was odd, though.’

‘The towel?’

‘No, not the towel particularly – though now I come to think of it, it was a bit small. If *I* was taking a hotel towel, I’d use a bath one, not a hand one. And taking a towel at all is odd if you’re intending to commit suicide. You’re not exactly expecting to be around to dry yourself off afterwards, are you? But no, it wasn’t that, there was something else. I remember looking down and thinking something wasn’t right, but I couldn’t place it then. I know now, though. I’ve just realised.’

‘What?’

‘The shoes.’

‘What shoes?’

‘That’s just it. There weren’t any shoes!’

‘Ah. Yes, we noticed that, too. Why do you think that’s odd? People do sometimes go barefoot, you know.’

‘Not on this island, they don’t; not if they’ve got any sense. Certainly not to that bay. The path down from the clifftop is sharp grit, and if you cut across any of the country between the hotel and that headland, you have to cross areas of gorse and burnet rose; all that would cut your feet to ribbons without shoes.’

‘Mr Taylor would have known that?’

‘I should think so. He was here last year.’

‘Perhaps he wore shoes into the water and they slipped off the body.’

‘Something like flip-flops, you mean? Perhaps. But hardly Richard’s style. It’s just odd. Like the towel, and the swimming in the night. But I suppose death is always odd, isn't it?'

Robbie remembered the Sergeant's expression, and the quick glance he had exchanged with the constable, who was taking notes. He drank the last of his chocolate and went back to his letter.

*Well, perhaps it was an accident. But I'm sure there was something strange about the whole thing, the more I think about it, Hal. Why would Richard go out at some ungodly hour of the night, by himself, without shoes, to go swimming? He wasn't the type to go swimming at all, as far as I remember him from last year. Perhaps Mum was right — she said it might have been suicide, and that people do some strange things when they're that desperate.*

*Anyway, the body was taken over to the mainland on the ambulance boat with the doctor, and the two policemen eventually went back on the last ferry. I suppose there will have to be a proper post-mortem, and an inquest. Dad was relieved when the ambulance boat arrived — he'd been worried about what would happen if the weather got any worse. The wind and rain have been dreadful today, and the ferries have only just managed to get through. He didn't want to get stuck with the body if there were no boats running — I don't know what would have happened if they couldn't get it off the island. Perhaps they'd have had to keep it in one of the big freezers. Ugh! What a thought!*

*Enough to put you off speciality ice-cream for life.*

*One way and another, it's been a funny old day. I'm glad I'm not staying in the hotel – the atmosphere's been really peculiar, with half the guests not knowing what's happened, but mooning about the place because the weather's too bad to go out, and picking up bad vibes from the staff and the guests who do know. I bet dinner tonight was a real strain. Mum stayed on at the hotel to help, but I came back to the cottage and made my own supper. She got back really late, and hardly said a word, which is not like her at all.*

*I wish you were here. If there were two of us, I'm sure all this would be exciting, but as it is, it's just depressing, and a bit frightening somehow. I'll keep writing to let you know what's happening – please write back soon, to cheer me up, and I'll try to phone you tomorrow.*

*My love to your mum. I hope the fishing trips with Peter haven't been too gruesome. Don't let the bastard grind you down!*

Robbie got up and prowled restlessly round the room, reading through what he'd written. He tried to imagine Hal's reaction; mostly confusion, probably – he didn't think he'd made a very good job of explaining the situation, when he read the whole letter again. But it was too late, and he was too tired, to change any of it now. He went back to the table, picked up the pen and signed the bottom of the letter, then began to get ready for bed.

On his way back from the bathroom, he stood and

listened outside his mother's bedroom. There was no sound from inside, but he saw the line of light under her door, and wondered if she'd fallen asleep without turning it off. He raised a hand to knock gently on the door, but suddenly felt sure that she *was* awake, and even more sure that he couldn't face talking to her; not at the moment.

He went back into his bedroom, got into bed and turned out the light. Lying in the darkness, he went over the events of the morning once more, turning the memories and impressions over and over in his mind as he drifted in and out of consciousness.

When he finally sank into sleep, the images in his dreams picked up his memories, unravelled them, and rewove them into new patterns, rich and strange but still accepted as familiar. He was standing on the clifftop in bright sunshine, looking out over the bay but seeing nothing except the glare reflected from the water, dazzling his eyes. He looked down at his feet and saw that they were bare, and when he moved forward they sank deep into the pile of a carpet, stretching before him all the way to the water's edge. He was on the beach now, not on the cliff, and Richard was walking towards him, leaving footprints in the carpet. He wore trousers and a shirt, and didn't look like Richard any more because he'd changed into Rowan Atkinson playing Mr Bean, and he was standing on one leg and shouting, 'Give me my underpants!'

Robbie woke and sat up in bed, breathing heavily. He leaned over and switched on the bedside light, reached for his letter and the pen, and added a postscript.

***I've just realised something else that was odd about the clothes on the beach. You'd expect people to fold clothes in the order they take them off, wouldn't you? But this pile had the underwear at the bottom!***

He switched off the light, rolled over, and was asleep again almost immediately.

# CHAPTER 7

By the next morning, the weather had improved enough for the first ferry to arrive and dock without difficulty. The sky was still heavily overcast and rain fell in a steady drizzle, but there was no longer any wind to whip up the waves. The droplets of rain lightly dimpled the surface of a gently rolling swell, and the deck of the ferry rose and fell just enough to make the task of unloading provisions hazardous. Bernard watched anxiously as the men struggled to keep their footing on the slippery deck, but at last the task was successfully completed.

There were no day trippers arriving on the early boat on such a wet morning, and only a handful of passengers for the return trip to Guernsey. Bernard had half expected Sarah to be among them, but there was no sign of her. He watched the ferry pull away from the steps, and then turned back towards the harbour office.

Sarah had indeed intended to catch the ferry; she had refused the offer to accompany Richard's body on the ambulance boat the day before because the weather was so bad, and had felt afterwards that perhaps she should have gone. But this morning, although the weather had improved, she had decided after all to stay in the hotel with Paul; the old man was still in a state of shock, and there would be little she could do at the hospital on the mainland except wait endlessly in echoing corridors. There would be things to be dealt with soon enough, but for the moment Paul's needs took priority.

Paul, after the first dreadful convulsion of uncontrolled grief, had slipped into a state that Sarah already knew well. Not coma, nor trance, but a sort of waking paralysis of the mind. His eyes remained open and he responded physically to stimuli, but speech deserted him and his movements were clumsy and uncoordinated. The first time it had happened, soon after worsening arthritis had forced his retirement from the company, Sarah thought he had had a stroke. Now she knew that the fit would pass. There was nothing she could do to hasten his return to normal consciousness, but he seemed to be aware of her presence with him, and it went some way towards soothing his distress. So she held his hand and murmured words of comfort, intended to dispel his nightmares, but aimed almost as much at her own.

* * *

Robbie woke late, and when he went downstairs his mother had already finished her breakfast. She made him coffee while he ate cereal and toast, and then came to sit at the table with him while he drank it. He sensed her unease, and knew she was searching for words to tell him something. He didn't want her to find the words; he knew what she would say and he didn't want to hear it.

He gulped down the hot coffee, not caring that it burned on his tongue and in his throat, willing her not to speak before he could retreat back to his room. He stood, dragging his chair awkwardly backwards across the stone-flagged floor so that it squealed like fingernails on a blackboard. His mother stretched out a hand towards him, and he knew there was to be no escape after all.

'Sit down, Robbie, I want to talk to you.'

He replaced the chair and perched reluctantly on the edge of it. Claire looked down at her interlaced fingers as she spoke, and he was glad not to have to meet her eyes.

'I have to go to the mainland today, to see Edward. It's about something important, that you should know. So I thought I'd better tell you now.'

Edward Harding was an old friend of Claire's parents. He was also a solicitor. The silence stretched taut across the table between them as Claire twisted and untwisted her fingers. Robbie couldn't bear to wait for her to speak again.

'It's all right,' he said, knowing that it wasn't all right at all, 'you don't have to spell it out for me. You're getting a divorce.'

She raised her head and looked at him, and he wasn't prepared for the surprise on her face.

'Is *that* what you think?'

He shifted uneasily on his chair, torn between relief and anger. It didn't take long for the anger to win.

'Of course that's what I think! What the hell do you expect me to think, the way things are? You never stop rowing, you've moved out of the hotel, and now you tell me you're going to see a solicitor – and not Dad's. Why would you need to consult Edward if it's not for a divorce? Give me credit for a bit of intelligence, Mum – it's what you pay all those school fees for, after all.'

As he said it, he found himself wondering whether the school fees would continue if his parents did split up, and hated himself immediately for the selfishness of the thought. Claire's fingers were more relaxed now, and the words seemed to come to her more easily.

'I'm sorry, Rob. I didn't want you to worry, that's all, but I suppose not knowing has only made it worse for you. I should have told you earlier what was going on. It's not quite as bad as you must be thinking. There's no question of divorce – not yet. I just need to see Edward for advice about the exact terms of the island's lease.'

It was Robbie's turn to look surprised.

'The lease? What has the lease got to do with anything? And what can Edward tell you that Dad's solicitor couldn't?'

'That's the whole point. I need an independent opinion on what happens when we disagree. I want to find out exactly what your father could do on the island without my consent.'

'What does he want to do?'

'A lot of development. A marina, a casino, blocks of luxury flats. And the development of the big house into a second hotel complex – and I do mean complex. It would be big, and expensive, and include a nightclub and a disco and God knows what else.'

Robbie's reaction was immediate and vehement.

'But he *can't*! That would be just awful. I can't believe he'd actually want to do all that.'

'Well, I'm afraid he does. I couldn't believe it either, at first. But he really is serious about it all. And he says he can do it even if I oppose him.'

'Can he?'

'I don't think so. Not all of it, at any rate. He certainly can't develop the house without my consent, because I own that outright. But I don't know how much of the rest of it he could do. It depends on the terms of the lease. That's why I need to see Edward.'

'Is that what all the rows have been about?'

'Most of them.'

Robbie was silent for a while. Thoughts followed one another in rapid confusion until his head reeled with them.

*A casino! That would really bring the Addenbrookes and the Hendersons and their like crawling out of the woodwork. How can Dad possibly think of anything as gross as a nightclub on Longuey? Is he having a mid-life crisis? What will Mum do? She said 'not yet'. No divorce – not yet. Oh God, what a mess! The whole idea is just stupid. Where could you possibly put luxury flats, anyway?*

He grabbed that thought as it flitted past, and held on to it.

'Where on earth would he fit in all this new development? A marina in the harbour area, I suppose, but you'd need a bigger breakwater for a start. And there's no room anywhere for flats, not without ruining the beaches.'

'Yes there is. The old fort. He wants to use that site, and the whole stretch of land leading out towards the causeway.'

'He *can't*! Surely he can't – can he?'

'I don't know,' said Claire, and Robbie noticed the tiredness in her voice. He hung on to another thought that presented itself, and seemed to offer some comfort.

'It will all cost a fortune, won't it? Surely he'll never be able to raise the money.'

Claire stood up, and looked down at him with a strange expression on her face; the corners of her mouth twisted into a wry half smile.

'No,' she said, 'he won't. Not now.'

* * *

By mid-morning the rain had stopped, though the sky was still solidly grey with cloud. The later ferries had brought a sprinkling of day-trippers, but most of them stayed around the harbour area or clustered round the pub and shops. Only the most doggedly determined headed towards the beaches, to spread their towels on the still-wet sand and set up their picnics in forlorn hope of sunshine to come.

The beach leading to the ruined fort was never popular even on sunny days, because of its stony shingle and lack of swimming areas free of rocks and seaweed. Today it was completely deserted. Robbie stood looking out over the sweep of the beach from the top of the low cliffs that skirted it, and watched the oyster-catchers in their undisturbed possession of the rocky area at the water's edge. The path he stood on was also deserted. Half overgrown with bracken and scrub, it was not often traversed by even determined walkers. Most visitors to the island didn't know it was there; it wasn't marked on the map showing the main footpaths, and there was a more obvious route that led directly across the headland to the next beach. The point where Robbie's path diverged from the main one, to run closely along the edge of the cliff, was not at all obvious. It had become so overgrown that it required a real effort to scramble through the brambles and gorse and undergrowth, and reach the point where the track opened out again and became more recognisably a definite path. Robbie's jeans were sodden from the knees downwards where he had pushed through the wet bracken, and though the tough denim protected him from the assaults of nettles and briars, his legs were covered in scratches from the more vicious attack of sloe bushes.

He turned away from the view of the beach and continued along the path, which now began a long climb through a loose tangle of shrubs, up towards the headland where the cliff became steeper and more rugged. Before the path reached its highest point and began the steep and slippery descent on the other side, Robbie stepped over a twisted tree-root beside the track and struck off into the undergrowth. Within yards he had reached what looked like an impenetrable wall of dense gorse-bushes, but he ducked under an overhanging branch and wriggled through a gap where no gap had seemed possible.

The tunnel, whose entrance was now so effectively masked by the gorse, had once been part of silver workings. In the Occupation years the first German garrison discovered the mine-shaft, long abandoned since the meagre seam ran out. They opened it out and extended the tunnel until it emerged at the cliff face, intending to use it as a gun emplacement. It was meant to be completed at the same time as the new fortifications at Fort Le Coq, but time passed and plans changed; a new garrison commander received orders to abandon the work and withdraw most of his men, as Longuey was no longer considered to be of major strategic importance and the main fortifications were to be concentrated on Alderney. The tunnel was never sealed off, but in the years of neglect before the island's post-war resettlement the gorse took over and did an efficient job of camouflage.

For almost as long as he could remember, this had been Robbie's secret place. He had never found any evidence of anyone else's presence in the tunnel, so he assumed he was the only one to have stumbled across the entrance. Like the swimming bay in the early morning, it was marked in his mind as his own private territory – but even better than the bay, because there was always the chance that that would be invaded by other people. He had never told anyone about this place, not even Hal.

He followed the tunnel as it led downwards, steeply at first and then levelling out. It twisted and turned to begin with, where it had originally followed the line of the elusive seam of silver-bearing rock. Then he turned a corner and saw light ahead of him, and the slightly musty smell of the confined tunnel gave way to the clear tang of sea air.

The tunnel ended in a small chamber opening out directly into the cliff face. The first time Robbie had found this place, he had wondered why nobody seemed to have noticed it from outside, but when he next stood at the far end of the causeway and looked back up at the cliff, expecting to see an obvious cave entrance, he realised how well camouflaged it was. The cliffs at this end of the island were not smooth and sheer but rugged and scattered with outcrops. From most points along the beach and out along the causeway to the fort, the opening in the cliffs was effectively masked, either by rocky outcrops or by patches of vegetation. Robbie could see it, because he knew what he was looking for, but he doubted whether anyone else would realise what was there, except from a boat out at sea immediately opposite the entrance.

He settled down on the small patch of smooth rock floor at the mouth of the chamber, where he could look out over the sweep of the beach, or in the other direction to the causeway and the fort and on out to sea. The group of rocks far out beyond the fort was thick with birds and white with their droppings, and their distant cries provided a mournful counterpoint to his thoughts.

He hadn't realised until he wrote his letter just how much he was missing Hal. The finding of the body would have been an exciting adventure if Hal had been with him. Without Hal, the whole thing was just overwhelmingly depressing, and rather frightening. He couldn't go to his mother for comfort – there were too many conflicts in his feelings about her. He was still angry at her failure to tell him the full story about Bernard's plans. But now that he did know the main cause of the conflict between his parents, it didn't make anything any better; in fact if anything it made things worse. The sense of personal betrayal he already felt had now been widened to include a threat to the places he loved so much, even extending to this secret place that had been his refuge for so long.

All at once the clouds rolled back, and for the first time since Robbie arrived on Longuey the sun came out, bringing a pale golden glow to the beach and a sparkle to the water. It was as if the rays reached out and touched some secret spring within him, and he felt the tears, held back for so long, well up and spill over to trickle down his cheeks. He made no move to wipe them away, but sat completely still and let them flow in silence, until his view of the sunlit beach was so blurred it could no longer be cleared by blinking. Then, as the sunlight strengthened and the clouds continued to recede, he wrapped his arms around his legs, rested his head on his knees, and gave himself up at last to shuddering waves of weeping.

# INTERLUDE : APRIL 1944

Captain Hugo Von Essler strode across the headland above Fort Le Coq, heading for the farmhouse tucked into the corner of the main pasture field. He had made this journey across the top of the cliffs many times since his first arrival on the island, but he approached this particular visit to the farm with very mixed feelings. He always enjoyed the opportunity to get away from the main garrison quarters at the fort, slipping away from the disciplined pettiness of the military routine into the gentler world of a timescale revolving round the needs of a dairy herd. But his visits were always uneasy and his welcome at best ambiguous, and today he brought news that would not be well received.

The milk quota to be sent to Guernsey had been increased again, and the penalty for not achieving it was the prospect of having the farm 'inspected' by S.S. officers from the mainland. Hugo knew what the likely outcome of such a visit would be: the removal of the island couple who ran the farm, the installation of slave workers from the Organization Todt, and the requisitioning of the farm buildings for their S.S. guards.

The implications were ominous, for Hugo himself and for the small group of troops he commanded to man the fort and supervise milk shipments. If Todt workers were once installed, they would not long be confined to farm work. Before coming to Longuey, Hugo had been stationed for a short while on Alderney. He had seen for himself the massive fortifications, in all their strength and ugliness, imposed there in response to Hitler's call for 'an impregnable fortress' in the Channel Islands. He had no stomach for the Alderney slave camps, or the brutish methods of the officers who supervised them, and he had been heartily glad to find himself posted to the comparative haven of Longuey. Now there was no knowing how long the haven would last; how long it would be before this little island too was swamped in concrete and wire and artillery emplacements, built by half-starved Russians and Jews treated worse than animals. It wasn't for this that Hugo had thought he was willing to fight a war; he could hardly remember now what he *had* thought it was for, but it certainly wasn't this.

He was surprised when he reached the main farm building to find it deserted; he was familiar enough with the daily routine of the farm to have timed his visit for one of the gaps in the normal working day. He stood outside the door for a while, wondering whether to try the barn or the lower field. The decision was made for him when a figure emerged from the barn and hurried along the rough track towards him, a dog bounding at her heels.

It was a young woman; hardly more than a girl. She wore trousers and heavy boots, and a thick Guernsey sweater that she had probably knitted herself. Hugo remembered the first time he had seen her, in these same working clothes, and felt something of the same shock he had experienced then; that such a rough covering should enclose such frail beauty, like a chrysalis cradling a butterfly. Her features were fine almost to the point of fragility, and the dark eyes seemed enormous in such a pale, delicate face. Her thick dark hair, which Hugo had only seen before twisted into a knot on top of her head, fell loosely about her shoulders today, and there was something in her movements that spoke of an agitation beyond the normal pressures of farm work.

She set down the bucket she carried, and frowned at him.

'You come at a bad time, Herr Captain.'

'I'm sorry. I'll be as brief as I can, but my news won't wait. Is your husband here?'

'No. He's out fishing. He took the boat out on the morning tide.'

Hugo hesitated, and she shrugged and picked up the bucket to take it indoors.

'You can tell me. We share the work; we can share the bad news.'

'I didn't say it was bad news.'

'Is there any other kind?'

She listened in silence, sitting at the big wooden kitchen table, as he told her, spreading out the sheets of the official letter from Guernsey and going through the figures and estimates for the new quotas. When he had finished, she raised one hand to brush a strand of hair back from her eyes, and he thought how exhausted she looked. When she spoke, her voice was dull and lifeless.

'It's impossible.'

'I know.'

'They must know too. You can't make a herd increase its yield just by signing a piece of paper. They must know that; they're not stupid. Why do they demand the impossible?'

'Because demanding the impossible is what they do best. They're good at it, and they enjoy it.'

She looked up at him, surprised by the bitterness of his tone.

'It's not your fault,' she said gently. 'You've always treated us fairly. I don't blame you for any of this.'

Her voice suddenly broke, and she put her head in her hands so that he couldn't see her tears. He stood beside her and fought the impulse to put a comforting hand on her shoulder. She sobbed once, then angrily swept the back of her hand across her eyes, and regained control of herself.

'I'm sorry. I meant to be strong. I will be strong, soon enough. But it's just hard to accept that this will probably be the end. We built up this herd from nothing; that's why we chose to stay with it when everyone else was evacuated. I love this place, and I love these animals, and I don't want to have to leave.'

'I know.'

Again, there was something in his voice that surprised her.

'Yes,' she said slowly, 'I really think you do.'

Hugo sat beside her and gathered up the sheets of the letter.

'It's not over yet,' he said, trying to convince himself as much as her. 'There might still be something I can do. You're quite right; they're not stupid. This isn't just about milk quotas, it's about the S.S. throwing their weight around. Well, they don't *always* get their own way. They can sometimes be out-manoeuvred.'

'What are you going to do?'

'I'm going to write a letter. These instructions were sent from a Major in the Todt Labour Organization. I'm going to send a letter, with a full report on your herd and its maximum yield, to a Lieutenant Colonel in the Military Command on Guernsey. If I can manage it without making him feel he's being manipulated, I'll also stress the insignificance of Longuey as a long-term strategic site. He's a reasonable man – but, more to the point, I happen to know he has a particular interest in cattle – and no great love of the S.S.'

'I see what you mean about the Major being out-manoeuvred.'

'Not so much out-manoeuvred as outranked.'

She smiled at him, and he managed to smile back. She wasn't stupid herself; she probably realised it wasn't as easy as he'd tried to make it sound. If it was really that easy he would already have done it – he had thought of it before but always been too aware of the risks involved. He was painfully conscious of the fact that rank extends in two directions, and an S.S. Major would make a powerful enemy. But now that he had made a decision he found himself strangely exhilarated.

The urgent barking of the dog somewhere outside reminded him of her preoccupation with other worries when he arrived.

'You said it was a bad time. You have other troubles, I think? Out in the barn?'

She nodded, and got up from the table.

'A difficult calving. It should have been straightforward, but something's wrong and I'm not sure that I can deal with it myself.'

'And your husband's out fishing.'

It wasn't meant as a criticism, but she flushed and became defensive.

'He couldn't know. There were no danger signs when the labour started. There should have been no problems. These things happen, that's all.'

'When do you expect him back?'

'Not until late tonight.'

'And by then you could have lost the calf?'

She nodded miserably.

'Not just the calf. The mother, too. She's getting more exhausted by the minute.'

Hugo became brisk and decisive.

'Then we mustn't waste time. Get the water you came back to the house to fetch, and then show me.'

When he felt gently inside the cow's vagina and along the flank of the calf, he understood at once why the girl had been unable to do anything about the problem. He had no doubt that she had the necessary knowledge of what was needed, and he suspected that there was surprising strength in that deceptively frail-looking figure, but what she lacked was reach. The calf was stuck because it had one leg folded right back from the shoulder, and Hugo was at full stretch as he reached for the foot to pull it round. Once the leg was in the right place the birth was amazingly quick and easy. Hugo looked up and caught the look of astonishment and admiration on the girl's face, and felt enormously pleased with himself.

'There! That's all the help she needed. A fine bull-calf! They'll do very nicely without me from now on.'

He saw the astonishment still lingering on her face, and laughed.

'We're not all born in uniform, you know. I was brought up on a farm. I might even have become a farmer, perhaps; once, a lifetime ago, without this war.'

There was a long silence before she replied.

'And after the war?'

Hugo shrugged.

'After the war, who knows? Who knows when it will end – or how? Impossible to think ahead. For all of us, there is only now. As there is for this little one.'

The calf was already trying feebly to stagger to its feet, as the cow licked it encouragingly. The girl bent to wipe it down with a wisp of straw, and her hair fell forward over her face.

'There might not have been a now for him at all, without you. Thank you, Herr Captain.'

He tried to respond with the formality his position imposed on him, but he caught the look of joy on her face as she turned back towards him, still cradling the wriggling calf in her arms, and he could not keep the sheer pleasure of the moment from showing in his voice.

'I'm delighted I arrived at the right time, Fräulein.'

'Annette,' she said, so softly that he could hardly hear her. 'My name is Annette.'

# CHAPTER 8

With the re-emergence of the sun, the island returned to some semblance of normality. The police tapes barring the entrance to the bay had been removed, and visitors once more disported themselves on the beach and in the water, in blissful ignorance of the sombre events of the previous day.

Robbie would normally have spent such a sunny afternoon on one of the beaches, but he found that his enthusiasm for swimming had completely disappeared. Claire had gone to Guernsey on the mid-morning ferry, and he was glad of her absence, but he was reluctant to stay in the cottage. He made himself sandwiches for an early lunch, and then went to the hotel to find his father. He didn't quite know what he would say to him, but he felt the time had come to say something, even at the risk of starting a major row. Anything would be better than this vague unease and restlessness.

In the event, his resolve came to nothing. Bernard was not available. He was closeted in his office in what the girl at the reception desk described as an Important Meeting, and was not to be disturbed. Robbie went into the lounge, chose a book from the bookshelf and took it out onto the front lawn, where he sank into one of the loungers set out invitingly facing the sun.

* * *

In the office, Bernard was struggling to maintain some authority in a conversation largely dominated by Neville Blythe.

'You realise, of course, that the whole situation is very delicate. I simply can't afford even the smallest risk of any of this becoming public.'

'I'm sure you know you can rely on my discretion. I've always ...'

'Yes, yes, I know, Bernard. You've always done everything in your power to protect my privacy. Don't think I'm not grateful for that – after all, it's one of the main reasons I've kept coming back here. But this is rather different. The question now is whether everything in your power will turn out to be sufficient. The police are involved, remember, and there will have to be an inquest.'

'There's no reason why you should have to have anything to do with that.'

'Not directly, no. But inquests, even in an out-of-the-way place like this, can attract the attention of the press. And once their attention is attracted, it can uncover all sorts of other things best left undisturbed. In the circumstances, Bernard, I think it would be wise to postpone our business connections.'

'Postpone?'

'Oh yes. I see no reason to abandon the scheme altogether. Even without Richard, it's still a very promising enterprise. But as things are, I'm certainly not willing to commit anything to paper at this stage. And I must make one thing perfectly clear. If there is the slightest hint of any scandal emerging that might impinge even remotely on me, I shall sever my connection with you entirely and take steps to protect my own interests – even if that proves to be at your expense.'

'Are you threatening me, Neville?'

'My dear Bernard, of course not. There's no need to be so melodramatic. I'm sure this whole unfortunate incident will blow over without any more fuss. But if it doesn't …'

'What?'

'Well, shall we just say, I'll make certain that it won't be *me* that will have awkward questions to answer.'

*  *  *

'Don't *fuss,* Sarah! I shall be perfectly all right. You go off and do whatever it is you have to do. I'm feeling much better now, and the sun will do me good. I'm not exactly an invalid, you know.'

Robbie looked up from his book as Sarah installed Paul in the lounger beside him, tucking a rug round his knees. She took a few steps back towards the hotel drive, hesitated, and returned to speak to Robbie.

'Are you going to be staying here for a while, Robbie?'

'Yes,' he said reluctantly, guessing what was coming next.

'I wonder – would you mind keeping Mr Taylor company until I get back? I have to go and make some telephone calls. I won't be long, but I'll feel happier if I know someone's with him.'

'Of course, Mrs Taylor.'

'Thank you, Robbie.'

She left them, and there was an embarrassed silence for a

while as Robbie wondered if he was expected to make polite conversation. Paul's first words surprised him.

'Has she gone?'

Robbie looked over his shoulder and saw Sarah just disappearing through the front door.

'Yes, she's gone into the hotel.'

Paul threw the rug off his knees with a sigh of relief. He saw Robbie's amused glance and smiled ruefully back at him.

'She's a wonderful woman, and I'm really grateful for all she does for me,' he said, 'but I wish she didn't do it quite so remorselessly. She'll *make* me an invalid if I let her.'

Robbie smiled in sympathy but couldn't think of anything to say. Paul looked at him shrewdly.

'It's all right, lad. You needn't feel obliged to make conversation. Go back to your book, if you like. I can see you were trying to find peace and quiet, before she descended on you. I won't disturb you.'

Robbie felt himself warming to this old man who could stay sensitive to the feelings of others in spite of all his own troubles. He closed his book and put it down on the grass beside him.

'It's all right,' he said, 'I wasn't really concentrating on the book, anyway. I'm quite happy to talk, if you like.'

'Books don't really help much, do they? I used to find that, too. You think it will help to take your mind off things if you bury yourself in a book, but it doesn't. I don't even try, these days; my eyesight's not up to much in the way of reading. You were the one who found Richard's body, weren't you?'

'Yes,' muttered Robbie, avoiding Paul's eye.

'It's all right, you needn't feel awkward about it; it won't upset me, not now. I'm sorry it had to be you. It can't have been a pleasant experience.'

'No, it wasn't.'

'I hear you kept your head, though; did all the right things. I'd like to thank you for that. If you hadn't raised the alarm so promptly we might have had to wait for the body to be washed ashore somewhere else eventually, perhaps much later.'

'That would have been awful. At least now you know. Not knowing would have been worse, wouldn't it?'

'It's always best to know,' agreed Paul, 'however bad it is. Then you can face up to things, and carry on.'

They both fell silent. Robbie thought how strange it was that the old man's words should echo his thoughts on his own situation so closely. When Paul spoke again, the shock of recognition was even stronger; it was as if the words had been plucked out of Robbie's own mind.

'I love this place! I hope it never changes.'

'So do I!' said Robbie vehemently, 'but I'm afraid it will, all the same.'

'I wouldn't be too sure about that. It's recovered from changes in the past. It will resist them now, you see if it doesn't.'

'You talk as if the island has a will of its own.'

'Well, hasn't it? It certainly has a character of its own – and a sort of magic. I'm sure you feel that.'

'Yes, I do,' said Robbie, surprised and a little confused, 'but I didn't think …' He fell into an awkward silence. Paul laughed softly.

'You didn't think I would? I do, you know; I feel it very strongly.'

'Even on a first visit?'

Paul didn't reply, but leaned forward to pull the rug back up over his knees, and Robbie turned to see Sarah advancing on them across the lawn.

‘I should escape now, if I were you,’ said Paul under his breath. Robbie bent to retrieve his book, and when he stood up Sarah was closer to them and Paul’s voice was loud enough for her to hear.

‘Thanks for your company, Robbie. I’ll be fine now – don’t let us make you late for your game of tennis.’

Sarah came up behind Paul’s chair, so missed the wink he gave Robbie.

‘Goodbye, sir. Perhaps we can chat again sometime.’

‘I’d like that,’ said Paul, and there was genuine pleasure in his voice. Robbie smiled down at him.

‘So would I,’ he said, and set off across the lawn.

It was only when he reached the gate out of the hotel grounds that he suddenly grinned, realising that for Sarah’s benefit he should have gone the other way, towards the tennis courts.

# CHAPTER 9

Sergeant Edward Harris swore under his breath and reached for the Tippex. Typing had never been his favourite occupation, and he always hated the laborious process of producing a legible report; he'd much prefer to be out and about than stuck in the St Peterport office, especially on a sunny day like today. Still, he had to admit that it did help to get an overall perspective on the case, having to sum it all up and translate Constable Brouard's typed-up notes into decent English. As he read through them again now, he felt once more the slight prickle at the back of his neck that he'd experienced when they'd been interviewing the boy. He couldn't put his finger on exactly what had aroused his suspicion; it was more a gut feeling that there was a good deal more to this death than met the eye. There was a certain amount of good-natured banter within the station about Ted Harris's gut feelings, since his figure was far from sylph-like, but there was a good deal of respect as well; the general opinion seemed to be that you didn't knock around for as long as Ted without developing a nose for when things were a bit dodgy.

He was feeling it now; that sixth sense that told him there was something fishy here. He'd only felt it briefly before, in his interview with the boy, but now it grew stronger as he read through the statements again and tried to fit them together into an overall picture.

He was interrupted by a knock at the door. The Inspector, as usual, didn't wait for an answer, but opened the door immediately and stuck his head round it.

'How are you doing, Ted? Got everything you need to sew this one up?'

Harris looked up from the keyboard with a frown.

'Hardly.' he said, but offered no further explanation. Inspector Le Sauvage came into the room and closed the door behind him.

'No problem, surely? Straightforward accidental death, isn't it? We've seen enough of them over the years. Idiots who never take any exercise, and know sod-all about the sea, come on holiday and behave like raving lunatics. I'm only surprised more of them don't end up dead.'

Harris shook his head.

'Not as simple as that this time, sir. At least, I don't think so.'

'Bugger!' said the Inspector. Harris waited, but nothing more was forthcoming. He sighed, and leaned back in his chair.

'I know I'm going to regret asking this, but what's the problem?'

Le Sauvage pulled up a chair and sat down.

'Not a problem, exactly, Ted. More of a nuisance, really.'

'You've got the Chief Super breathing down your neck?'

'More than just breathing down it; applying a stranglehold. He's let it be known he wants this one cleared up as quickly and simply as possible.'

'Meaning ...?'

'Meaning he'd like a straightforward verdict of accidental death with no request from us for an adjournment of the inquest. He didn't actually say that in so many words ...'

'No, he wouldn't.'

'..but that was what he meant. I was left in no doubt.'

'Any idea why?'

Le Sauvage hesitated, but only briefly. He'd worked with the Sergeant for long enough to know he could trust his discretion.

'Pressure from on high. Words have been quietly exchanged on the golf course. Someone on Longuey wants to keep a low profile, and has some very influential friends.'

Harris gave a grin that exposed nicotine-stained teeth.

'I know just who that will be!'

Le Sauvage looked at him sharply.

'There hasn't been an attempt to nobble you, has there, Ted?'

'No, no – nothing like that. But I saw the hotel register, and I saw Martel's list of names from the original bookings, and I noted which names didn't match. There's a couple of 'Mr & Mrs Smith' registrations, actually, but one of them is particularly interesting, if you read your Hansard.'

'Ah. Well, you see the pressure that puts us under.'

Harris grinned again.

'Puts you under, you mean. Nothing to do with me. I don't play golf with the Commissioner. I just do my job.'

He did understand only too well the difficulties the Inspector was facing, but for the time being he was enjoying playing the innocent. He wondered if Le Sauvage knew the full extent of the problem; he rather doubted it. He wouldn't have worked it out himself if it hadn't been for the constable's sharp eye, but when Brouard spotted the girl it hadn't taken long to put two and two together – or one and one, to be more precise. Constable Brouard was a good lad, even if his written English did still leave a lot to be desired. He'd seen Abigail in the lounge of the hotel, and said immediately, 'Isn't that the Meredith girl, sir? You know, father in the Cabinet, scholarship to Cambridge, brief flutter with one of the junior Royals; then there was that drugs bust last year she managed to wriggle out of by the skin of her teeth; Daddy's influence, I bet that was. What's she doing in this neck of the woods?'

Harris had just been asking himself the same question about Neville Blythe, and the two questions had dovetailed neatly into one another. No wonder there was pressure being brought to bear now; he could imagine what panic the thought of a police investigation must have triggered in Blythe, who was widely tipped for the post of Environment Minister in the next re-shuffle and could do without any hint of scandal.

The Inspector was looking uncomfortable, and it wasn't just because he was sitting on the hardest chair in the office.

'I'm not asking you to cut any corners, Ted. I'm just passing on a general message, that's all. We've been asked for maximum discretion on this one.'

'Right you are, sir,' said Harris innocently, 'Message received and understood. Don't really know what you're worrying about, though. Always discreet, me.'

He savoured the look of apprehension that flitted across the Inspector's face. Le Sauvage must know that a request for discretion was only likely to increase his determination to get at the whole truth. The Inspector shuffled on his chair.

'You said it wasn't simple. What's the complication?'

'Several things. It doesn't quite add up. The preliminary post-mortem report, for a start. It's drowning, all right, but there are some odd features; not as much water in the lungs as you'd expect ...'

'That's not necessarily a problem,' interrupted the Inspector. 'You know as well as I do, Ted, a drowning doesn't *have* to leave a lot of water in the lungs. You've sat through enough inquests to know about 'dry' drowning – where the muscles of the larynx go into spasm almost immediately and prevent much water getting through. This could just be one of those.'

'Could be, sir, I suppose. But it isn't only that. There's a lot of heavy bruising around the shoulders, and substantial damage to the ribs – difficult to say in both cases whether caused before or after death. Some very odd marks on the face, too.'

'Hardly surprising, surely. Bodies get battered in the sea, that's all.'

'Perhaps.'

'Anything else?'

'Not specifically. I just find it hard to buy the idea of a swimming accident, that's all. From what nearly everybody's said about him, he wasn't the type to go swimming at all, let alone in the middle of the night. And the suicide theory is a bit of a non-starter, as well, from what we've got so far. No money worries, no business problems, no domestic upsets.'

'As far as you know. Don't be too quick to give up on the domestic angle, Ted. You know as well as I do, there can be a lot going on under the surface.'

Harris grinned again, and leaned even further back in his chair. He was beginning to enjoy himself.

'Go for suicide, then, is that it? But wouldn't that be almost as embarrassing for your golfing buddies as a full investigation? Bring the gutter press sniffing around immediately, that would; suicide of prominent businessman in holiday retreat. No, to have any hope of escaping notice it would have to be a straightforward tragic accident. And unfortunately for the Chief Super, I'm afraid that's exactly what it isn't.'

Le Sauvage sighed and stood up.

'All right, Ted. I'll tell him we'll probably have to ask for an adjournment.'

'Rather you than me!'

'Don't rub it in.' He hesitated with his hand on the door handle, 'I suppose there might still be an outside chance it will turn out to be accident after all?'

'Ask me again when I've seen the full post-mortem report. But I shouldn't bank on it. If you really want to know, I think it's much more likely that you'll end up as Investigating Officer in a suspected murder case.'

Le Sauvage said nothing, but his shrug spoke volumes.

'Don't worry,' said Harris cheerfully to his Inspector's retreating back, 'You know we make a great team.'

* * *

It was late in the afternoon before Robbie found the opportunity to speak to his father. Bernard had been frantically busy all day, but Robbie finally tracked him down to the cramped little office in the smallest of the buildings around the harbour, where the administration was done for all movements of boats. The tenancy of Longuey included the equivalent of the post of harbour-master, as well as primary responsibility for maintaining law and order. Even without any extra problems, the task of keeping the island running smoothly was a huge and complicated one. Robbie was used to finding his father preoccupied with the pressures of the job, but he wasn't prepared for the look of sheer exhaustion on

Bernard's face as he sat slumped on his chair now, his jaw slack and his eyes staring unseeingly out of the tiny window. There was a greyish tinge to his skin and dark shadows under his eyes; with a shock that made him shudder, Robbie suddenly saw his father as old.

Bernard pulled himself together, but not without Robbie noticing what an effort it took him.

'Hello, Rob. I thought you'd be on the beach on a day like this.'

'I wanted to talk to you. Mum's gone to see Edward today. Did you know?'

'Yes, I knew.'

There was an awkward silence. Now that the moment had come, Robbie was strangely reluctant to speak. He'd been gearing himself up all day to tackle his father and bring things out into the open, but now it felt dreadful to think of adding to the burdens that were already having such an obvious effect on him. In the event, it was Bernard who made the first move.

'I'm sorry, Rob. I should have talked to you before; come to find you, not let you trail around looking for me. It's Richard's death – it's been such a shock, and it's thrown up so many complications. But that shouldn't be any excuse, really. Your mother said I ought to find time to talk to you, and she was right.'

'She usually is,' said Robbie. He didn't mean it to sound aggressive, but that was the way it came out.

'What has she told you?'

'Enough. That you want to build a marina. And flats. That's bad enough; but a casino, and a nightclub … how could you, Dad? You know the way she feels about Longuey. The way I feel, too. I thought you understood. But now you seem to want to turn it into exactly the sort of place we can't stand, full of the sort of people that make us want to throw up.'

Bernard gave a wry smile.

'You do have a way of going right to the point, don't you? I do understand all that, as a matter of fact. I even feel the same way, to a certain extent. But it's not as simple as that, Robbie. Nothing ever is, I'm afraid. I can't make your mother see that, either, but it's true. We can't ignore pressures for change, even in a place like this. We've got to be prepared to adapt, or we'll eventually go under.'

'What do you mean? We're not in financial trouble, are we?'

'Not immediately, no. But I can see the possibility looming in the future, and we can't afford to leave it until it's more than a possibility. I've got to plan ahead, and those plans have got to include development.'

'Development means change. I don't want things to change. Why can't we stay the way we were?'

Bernard's voice was gentler now, and he looked Robbie directly in the eyes.

'You're not talking about the island now, you're talking about us. But it's the same principle, Robbie. People don't stay the same; they change, they grow, they develop. And relationships have to develop, too, or they die. It can be painful, but it's necessary.'

Robbie found himself thinking of Hal and his step-father, and the fishing trip. He struggled to contain his anger, but failed.

'I don't believe you!' he said, his voice shaking, 'I don't believe it's necessary to do all those beastly things to the island, when you know how much it will upset Mum. But you're right about people changing. *You've* changed. When you talked about the island, you used to sound like Grandpa.

Now you sound just like Henderson, and Addenbrooke's father.'

'Who are Henderson and Addenbrooke?' asked Bernard.

'It doesn't matter. I just hate them, that's all.'

Bernard ran one hand through his hair and massaged the back of his neck, and Robbie thought that he'd never seen anyone look so tired.

'Robbie, you're not making much sense. Can't we leave this for today? We've all had a tough time in the last couple of days, and we're too stressed to think clearly. But I'm not just fobbing you off. I promise we'll talk properly about all this soon. We shouldn't have kept you in the dark for so long; we won't in future. All right?'

'I suppose so,' muttered Robbie doubtfully, turning to leave the office.

'It will all be all right in the end, you'll see.'

'Yes.'

Neither of them sounded as if they believed it.

Robbie went back to the cottage, leaving Bernard sitting motionless at his desk staring abstractedly into space.

* * *

Sergeant Harris read through the completed notes on the interviews and added them to the file. Then he took out the preliminary post-mortem report and read it again. He sat for a while absent-mindedly tapping a pencil against the side of the bottle of Tippex.

'Why not?' he said aloud, reaching for the telephone and dialling a number. 'No harm in being prepared in advance. I may be wrong, but then again, who knows?'

He reached for a sheet of paper as he listened to the ringing tone, and doodled a line of pencil footprints along one edge, and then a little boat in the top right-hand corner. The ringing continued for a long time, and he added an elaborate question mark underneath the boat and began to decorate its outline with little asterisks. Just as he was about to give up, the phone was answered.

'Sorry to bother you, Mr Martel. Rather tedious routine enquiry, I'm afraid. Could I trouble you to let us have a complete list of all boats moored off Longuey for any of the last three days? You can send us a written copy for confirmation, but I'd quite like the information now, if that's possible; that's why I rang the harbour office number instead of the hotel. I had a hunch you might be there this afternoon.'

By the time he rang off, Harris had filled half the sheet of paper with names of boats, and the asterisks had completely eclipsed the original shape of the question mark.

# CHAPTER 10

The detailed post-mortem report, including the results of the lab tests on various samples, had come in first thing in the morning, and Harris found a copy of it on his desk when he arrived for duty. He read through it rapidly, then re-read one particular section more carefully, nodded in satisfaction, and headed for Inspector Le Sauvage's office.

The Inspector was just replacing the telephone receiver as Harris came into the room, and looked none too pleased to be interrupted. Harris plunged in regardless.

'Have you seen the full autopsy report, sir?'

'Yes.'

'The measurements of the feet don't match the footprints.'

'I know.'

'You realise it means he probably went into the water from a boat, not from the shore at all?'

Le Sauvage waved Harris to a seat, and sat down himself.

'Yes, Ted, I do realise exactly that. It's hardly a surprise to you anyway, I would have thought – isn't that the way you were already thinking?'

'It's a logical next step from doubting the swimming

accident story, yes. But it leads to some very awkward implications, especially in view of all those requests for discretion you were getting. There's been a definite attempt at a cover-up here, sir, and I don't like it; I don't like it one little bit.'

'All right, Ted – calm down. There's no need to get aggressive with me. I agree with you.'

'You do?'

'Of course I do. I trust your instincts on this one; you weren't happy with it from the beginning, were you?'

'You didn't sound like someone who trusted my instincts when we last talked. You sounded like someone who wished I'd shut up and behave myself.'

Le Sauvage smiled briefly, but without enjoyment.

'Fat chance of that! When was the last time you behaved yourself, Ted? No, I knew you'd press on regardless. I just hoped you'd turn out to be wrong this time, that's all; it would have made my life much easier. But now I think you may be right about the cover-up. Somebody's been trying to make fools of us, and I resent that just as much as you do, believe me.'

'Too right, I resent it! What sort of idiots do they take us for, feeding us folded clothes on a rock and lines of footprints – it's like something out of Agatha Christie. I don't appreciate being set up, and I don't like conspiracies.'

'That's a bit strong, isn't it? Someone's been lying, certainly, but does it have to be more than one? Why not just a killer attempting to cover his tracks?'

Harris considered this thought at length, but finally shook his head doubtfully.

'Could be, sir, I suppose. But it just doesn't feel like that to me. It feels like group panic; people going into a huddle and thrashing about for a way out, and coming up with something melodramatic without thinking it through.'

'Could still be panic with only one person.'

'I know. I'm just telling you what it feels like to me, that's all.'

'Well, all right – so now we've got to get down to the nitty gritty of finding out whether you're right or not. Start from scratch and go through all the evidence, in detail and by the book.'

'We'll have to have it all watertight for your golf-playing buddies. They're not going to be too happy about all this.'

Le Sauvage looked at him sharply.

'Come off it, Ted. That chip on your shoulder's getting a bit too obvious. We want it all watertight for *us*, never mind them. You didn't really think I'd be willing to go along with hushing it up once we knew it was a suspicious death, did you?'

Harris had the grace to look sheepish, and the Inspector didn't wait for a reply.

'From now on, there's no question of anybody – and I mean *anybody* – getting kid-glove treatment.'

'Even members of Her Majesty's Government?'

'Even members of Her Majesty's royal bloody family, if necessary – though I don't think we've actually got any of those skulking about the islands anywhere. Unless, of course, you know something I don't?'

There was a short but telling silence before Harris spoke.

'Was that a bow drawn at a venture, or has Brouard been babbling?'

'Neither. I do my homework, that's all. The young lady covers her tracks very effectively, I grant you, but she's too highly connected to move through these waters without leaving any ripples – especially since her little flutter with the House of Windsor last year.'

'Well, I'll be damned!' said Harris ruefully, 'and here was I thinking I'd got an exclusive, thanks to young Brouard's sharp eye for a face. But hang on a minute – surely if her presence here is no secret after all, we can rule her and Blythe out of the reckoning as far as the need for a cover-up is concerned.'

'I wouldn't go so far as to say her presence is no secret, Ted. There are secrets and secrets. *You* know she's here, and *I* know she's here, and so do one or two other very unobtrusive and discreet people. But the gentlemen of the press certainly don't know she's here, and neither does her father. I wouldn't like to bet one way or the other on Blythe's wife. In any case, even if they don't care who knows they're here, that doesn't necessarily get us very far. It depends what they've been up to, and whether there's any connection with the death. They might be completely innocent …'

'Or they might both be in it right up to their eyeballs!'

'Exactly. So we treat them both as potential suspects until they're eliminated, exactly the same as anyone else. Except …'

'Except what, sir?'

'Don't take this the wrong way, Ted; I know you did all the preliminary work, but when it comes to interviewing this time round, I'd rather handle these two myself. No kid gloves, but there's no need for dirty great boxing mitts, either!'

Harris tried out his hurt expression, but he knew it wasn't convincing. He was actually relieved to have the responsibility taken out of his hands; he wasn't sure that he'd have trusted himself to treat Blythe impartially. It was one of his failings, and he was uncomfortably aware of it. He'd overheard one of the other Sergeants in the canteen once: 'The trouble with our Ted is, he can suffer fools as gladly as you like, but it's the clever bastards he can't stand!' He'd joined in the laughter, but uneasily, the truth behind the joke tugging at his conscience like a fingernail probing a scab.

'Fine by me, sir – they're all yours, and I wish you joy of them.'

Le Sauvage reached for a file on his desk, and Harris rose to leave the office. The Inspector's voice stopped him before he reached the door, conversational but with a definite edge to it.

'By the way, Sergeant, why did you feel the need to keep Miss Meredith's presence to yourself? If you'd mentioned it to me earlier you could have saved me the trouble of finding out for myself.'

Harris turned back and looked the Inspector straight in the eye.

'Only following your directions, sir.'

'In what way, Sergeant?'

'I was being discreet, sir,' said Harris, and escaped before Le Sauvage could reply.

* * *

The first meeting in the incident room was cramped and rather hurried. Le Sauvage had called a temporary halt to the bustle of physical activity involved in getting the room ready, to hold a preliminary briefing. It was a bit like holding a site meeting in some sort of surreal warehouse; the exercise equipment normally stored in the big room was still being moved out as the banks of computer terminals and the office furniture were moved in, and the sudden demand for a cessation of activity had left telephone cables draped in sinister loops everywhere. The investigating team perched where they could and listened in silence as the Inspector filled them in.

'Right, it's official; this is now a suspicious death, possibly a homicide. There were always snags with the scenario of a straightforward swimming accident, and now the detailed autopsy report gives us enough grounds for suspicion to open a full investigation. Cause of death is still drowning, but there are two things in particular that make it look less like an accident. First, as well as the normal battering a body always gets in the water, there are unusual marks on the face; tiny abrasions like pin-pricks clustered close together, and in some places extending into scratches. Similar marks on the shoulder, but much less prominent. Secondly, the detailed measurements of the feet of the body don't match the footprints in the sand – even allowing for the fact that the prints had been blurred by the rain by the time we got to them. Also, the forensic report on the clothes on the beach strongly suggests that they were never actually worn; the shirt in particular was still folded as if it had just come straight from the laundry. All of that adds up to suspicious circumstances. I know Ted has a theory about the death, so I'll give him his moment of glory and let him tell you what he thinks at this stage.'

Harris scowled, wondering if the Inspector was indulging in sarcasm, but spoke out confidently nevertheless.

'The footprints are phoney – he went in off a boat, not from the shore at all; that seems pretty obvious. If so, he can't have been alone, or the boat would still have been there when the body was found. That means there was at least one other person involved; *someone* shifted the boat away from the scene, someone made those footprints – which makes it likely that someone was there when he drowned. I'd go further than that myself; I think someone may well have prevented him from getting back on the boat – or even held him under.'

Le Sauvage nodded.

'Seems likely. In which case, the drowning itself could well have been murder. But we also have to consider three other main questions. First, how did he get into the water in the first place?'

'Did he fall or was he pushed?' muttered a sergeant with an unoriginal turn of phrase.

'Second,' went on the Inspector, pretending he hadn't heard, 'was he hauled aboard again at any stage? The relatively small amount of water in the lungs, and the severe bruising to the ribs, are consistent with an attempt at artificial respiration. The pathologist won't actually commit himself definitely on that, but it's a possibility to bear in mind. And third, if he went into the water from a boat, how did his clothes get on the beach and who made the footprints?'

Harris noticed the youngest of the constables earnestly taking notes, and was irresistibly reminded of the jury in "Alice in Wonderland" laboriously writing everything down on their slates. The Inspector glanced hastily at his watch and continued.

'We're unlikely to get first-hand evidence on any of this – there probably won't have been independent witnesses in the early hours of the morning. So we do it the hard way; build up a picture piece by piece. First line of enquiry; to establish deceased's exact movements on the day of the incident. This is going to be a tricky one – there are long stretches of time unaccounted for, and the location doesn't exactly lend itself to the standard approach. On Longuey, it's not so much house to house as kiosk to kiosk. Main target will be the hotel residents and staff, obviously, and there's a team going across to set up an interview room in the hotel itself. But we'll also have to attempt to track down any of the casual visitors to the island who might have noticed anything relevant, and that's not going to be easy. It was a sunny holiday Sunday; the day trippers were thick on the ground, and they will have come from all points of the compass. That's why I'm off to the studios in a few minutes time; we're putting out a radio and TV appeal for anyone who visited Longuey on that day to contact us. So first priority here is to get the phones set up and manned, because all hell will break loose from the minute the broadcasts go out. Most of it will be a waste of time, of course, but someone may come up with something useful.'

Harris voiced the question several of the team were thinking.

'Will we have enough man-power, sir?'

'For the time being, yes, I think so. We'll be spread a bit thin, but we can cope. We can even spare a couple of people to look into the other area of interest that springs to mind – the money. Richard Taylor was apparently a wealthy man, but it's a complicated situation; we need to know how much of his money was tied up in his company, and how much of an interest his father still had in the financial side of things – and we need to know the terms of his will, to find out who exactly inherits what and who might gain from his death. That gives us plenty to be going on with. Now, if there are no questions, I'll leave you to it and get off to the studio.'

He swept out of the room, and the activity was soon in full swing again.

Harris and Brouard rolled up their shirt sleeves and gave a hand with the furniture removals. When the last exercise bicycle had been manhandled into the storeroom, Harris collapsed on to a rolled up floor-mat and mopped his brow. Brouard surveyed him anxiously.

'Are you all right, sir? You've gone very red.'

Harris was breathing heavily, but his voice was steady enough.

'I'm fine. A bit out of condition, that's all.'

Brouard waved a hand at the exercise bicycles.

'Perhaps you should have a go on one of these occasionally. Keep you fit.'

Harris snorted.

'Not bloody likely! The only way to avoid injury is to refrain from physical exercise – like the only way to keep healthy is to stay away from doctors.'

Brouard perched himself on the edge of a table.

'Do *you* think somebody hauled him out and tried to revive him, sir?'

'Yes, I do. I think he was probably fully dressed when he went into the water. But he was in swimming trunks when the body was found. Think of the implications of that, lad.'

'Somebody took the clothes off him after he was dead?'

'Right – and then slipped him back into the water. I think I can see how it might have been. Never mind how he got into the water in the first place; once in, he'd have been in real difficulty almost immediately. It's hard enough getting back on board a boat from the water at the best of times. But he wasn't a good swimmer, from what we've been told. And he was drunk – not legless, but the post-mortem showed enough alcohol in his blood for his coordination to have been badly affected. He might easily have drowned anyway. But somebody made sure. Somebody held him under.'

'Then why haul him out again? Just to take the clothes off and make it look as if he'd gone swimming? And why attempt to revive him?'

Harris shrugged.

'Who knows? Could have been a change of heart by the attacker. Could have been other people intervening. In any case, I'm sure by that stage there was panic. A body on the boat; an unsuccessful attempt at resuscitation; some bright spark having the idea to make it look like a swimming accident. Ironic, really.'

'How come, sir?'

'Well, they would have done much better just leaving the body in the water from the beginning. It would have sunk, and by the time it washed up again it would have been difficult to tell where it went into the water. As it was, the attempt at a cover-up just made things worse, not better.'

Brouard frowned.

'Yes, but hang on, sir – that was just their bad luck that the body happened to get caught up in the fishing lines. Without that, it would still have sunk and not washed up until later. We might never have suspected anything, then.'

'Or perhaps they knew about the fishing lines and wanted the body found as soon as possible.'

'Could be, sir. It does sort of go together, doesn't it? – footsteps and clothes on the beach, body in the water.'

'In that case, I'll tell you one thing, lad; I hope to God Martel doesn't turn out to have been involved in this.'

'Why's that, sir?'

'He of all people would have known who'd be the first to arrive on that beach in the morning. What sort of man sets up his own son to discover a body?'

# CHAPTER 11

On Longuey, the holiday atmosphere had begun to re-assert itself among most of the hotel guests. Those who had been aware of the events of the previous days were if anything more animated than usual, as if intimations of their own mortality had made them determined to seize every moment of enjoyment while they could. The conversation in the dining room at breakfast was livelier than usual, and punctuated by bursts of laughter.

Robbie had walked all the way round the island after an early breakfast, taking the paths which kept closest to the sea and diverting on to each of the beaches. He often did this in the morning, before the first main load of holiday-makers arrived on the second ferry of the day. There were rarely many other people about; the hotel guests were usually still lingering over their breakfasts, and not many day-trippers came over on the first, early-morning ferry. He could enjoy the feeling that the whole island belonged only to him and the sea-birds, and the rabbits that occasionally scuttled ahead of him as he pushed his way through the bracken of the more overgrown sections of path.

This morning he'd met no-one, either on the paths or on his excursions on to the beaches. He'd wandered through rock pools, picked up shells along the high-water mark and skimmed flat stones across the water, managing for a short while to shut out all his worries and feel like a carefree child again.

Now, without making a conscious decision, he found himself heading for the hotel. As he walked up the path towards the front door he looked up and saw that Paul was sitting out on the balcony of his room, with a breakfast tray on the table beside him. Robbie waved up at him, and Paul waved back and called down,

'Good morning, Robbie. It looks as if it's going to be a beautiful day today, doesn't it?'

'Yes, sir, I think you're right.'

'You're out and about early. Have you been for a walk?'

'Yes – around the island.'

'Would you like to come and tell me about it? Come and share my breakfast. Unless you're busy, of course. I don't want to impose on your time.'

'No, it's all right – of course I'll come and talk to you if you'd really like me to. I've had breakfast already, thank you, but I'd love some orange juice if you've got any to spare.'

'Come on up, then. You'll find the door isn't locked, so come through to the balcony.'

Robbie half expected to find Sarah in Paul's room, but he was alone. As if reading his thoughts, Paul answered the unspoken question.

'Sarah's gone down to breakfast with the Wilson family. She didn't want to go, but I insisted. She's cooped up with me far too much, and it isn't really necessary. I know all this has been a terrible shock for both of us, but she'll have to get back to normal life eventually, and wrapping herself up in me isn't going to help – for her or for me. They're a nice family, the Wilsons. Jean has been very understanding.'

He poured a glass of orange juice from the jug on the table, and handed it over to Robbie.

'It's good to have company, though – even if I did tell Sarah I'd prefer to have breakfast alone for once; that was strictly for her benefit. Now, tell me about this walk of yours.'

'Not much to tell, really. All the way round the island, keeping as close to the shoreline as possible. There are obvious paths most of the way, but some of them are a bit overgrown, and there's one bit where it's just a scramble through the dunes and you pick your own route. I went down on to most of the beaches, too – they're often at their best in the early morning.'

Paul nodded in understanding.

'No people!'

'Yes. It's not just that, though. There's something about the quality of the light in the morning, before the sun really gets up. I love just watching the light on the water, especially when it's calm, like today.'

Paul's voice when he responded was surprisingly soft and dreamy.

'I know just what you mean. Not the brash, vulgar glitter you get in the heat of the day, but more of a soft glow. Like the difference between diamonds and opals. I always did prefer the semi-precious stones, myself. They have more soul, somehow.'

Robbie looked at him in wonder.

'That's it! That's it exactly. How do you do that?'

'Do what?'

'Put your finger right on what I'm thinking. You did it yesterday, too.'

Paul smiled.

'I think the same way, that's all. You remind me very much of myself when I was younger, Robbie. I expect we're just kindred spirits. Shall I tell you something else I think about the light on the water?'

'Yes.'

'I think you watch it in the evenings, too.'

'Yes. When the light's fading and the sea goes silver. Better than gold.'

'You watch the shimmer on the surface of the water, and you wouldn't be at all surprised to see mermaids.'

'Yes. How do you know?'

'I just know.'

There was a fragile silence between them for a moment, and then Paul casually broke the spell.

'Would you like more orange juice?'

'No, thanks, this is fine.'

The conversation seemed at the same time both natural and extraordinary. Robbie was amazed at the speed with which they seemed to have achieved the same level of rapport it had taken him years to reach with Hal. He felt completely at ease with Paul. No – it was more than that; more than just the feeling that he'd known him for a long time. There was a sense of shared experience. He could tell Hal things and know Hal would understand, but Paul seemed to understand already, without needing to be told at all.

'I saw a dolphin once,' Robbie said, 'on an evening just like that – when I was looking for mermaids. I was miserable, and I needed something magic, and then suddenly there it was; in the deep water out beyond the old fort. I watched it playing for a long time, and it was beautiful – when it finally headed out to sea, I wasn't miserable any more.'

'What was it you were miserable about?'

'I can't remember.'

'Then the magic worked!'

'I know. But I've never seen the dolphin again, though I've been in the same place lots of times since. Perhaps we're only ever allowed one piece of magic each, and I've used mine up. But I think the place has kept a little bit of it, all the same. I go there sometimes now. When I need to hide.'

He stopped, suddenly wary. He'd told Hal about the dolphin, but not where he'd seen it from. This was the closest he'd ever come to telling anyone about his secret place, and he felt that to confide in Paul would be somehow disloyal to Hal.

Paul looked at him gravely.

'I understand that, too,' he said, 'You're lucky to have a place to go to. When I need to hide, I have to do it inside my head; that's my secret place, the one that's supposed to protect me and make things better. It doesn't always work, though.'

'Nor does mine,' said Robbie, his voice trembling, and all at once he found himself spilling out the whole story: the lease, Bernard's plans, the rows between his parents, his own worries about a divorce – everything. He managed not to cry, but his throat tightened enough to make his voice sound very peculiar at times, and when he reached the end he desperately wanted to blow his nose. He fumbled in his pocket for his handkerchief, and in pulling it out he scattered sand and a handful of shells over the floor. Covered in confusion, he gave his nose a good blow and returned the handkerchief to his pocket, then sank to his knees and began to gather up the shells.

'I'm sorry. I didn't mean to embarrass you like this,' he muttered.

'My dear boy, I'm not in the least embarrassed. I'm glad you got it off your chest ... has it ever struck you what a silly expression that is, by the way? Wherever all of that came from, it certainly wasn't on your chest! But I hope you feel better for saying it, at any rate.'

'Yes, I think I do, actually.'

'Better out than in. Another silly expression!'

Robbie scrambled to his feet and put the rescued shells on the table.

'I'm sorry about all the sand on your floor.'

'No problem. I'm sure the chamber-maid will remove it very efficiently.'

Feeling much better, Robbie grinned.

'That's one thing this hotel is really good at – dealing with sand. We get enough practice – you'd be amazed how much of the stuff ends up in the laundry. I know – I've done my stint of cleaning it out of the washing machine filters.'

Paul leaned forward and picked up one of the shells.

'This one's lovely.'

'I like the scallop shells. I love the way they're never quite perfectly symmetrical; somehow it makes them more beautiful, not less. This one's not a very good colour, though. I've got better ones at home.'

Paul took something out of his waistcoat pocket and put it on the table; a tiny jeweller's box.

'Like this?'

He opened the box. Inside, nestling in cotton-wool like a brooch or a pendant, was a deep coral pink scallop shell.

Robbie looked at it in surprise. It seemed a strange thing for a wealthy retired businessman to be carrying around with him, though it was a beautiful shell; an almost perfect specimen.

Paul took out the shell and turned it over, his fingers caressing the smooth under-side.

'It's the contrast I like,' he said, 'I love the feel of the rough ridges on the outside, and then this wonderful silky smoothness inside. You're quite right about the symmetry. It would spoil the effect if the two halves did match exactly; you'd lose the feel of something that had once been living.'

He put the shell back in its cotton-wool nest, and returned the box to his pocket. When he spoke again, his voice was strong and decisive.

'It will all turn out all right in the end, you'll see,' he said. 'You have to make yourself believe that.'

'I'll try. My friend Hal says it's best to be a pessimist, because then you can only ever be pleasantly surprised. But I can't do that; I'm a natural optimist, really. It's just hard to keep it going, sometimes.'

'I know.'

Robbie was instantly reminded of Paul's own situation, and found himself covered in confusion.

'I'm sorry. What must you be thinking of me? I shouldn't be burdening you with all my troubles when …' His voice trailed off into silence.

'When I've got troubles enough of my own?' finished Paul gently. 'Yes, these are difficult times for all of us to get through. But Sarah's way isn't the answer. She's trying to ignore what's happened altogether, and if she goes on bottling it up much longer she'll be heading for a breakdown eventually. But at the same time she's deliberately making a martyr of herself, protecting and mollycoddling me until I think I shall go mad. It's a relief to talk to someone who's willing to bring problems out into the open – in a way, it doesn't really matter whose problems they are. And I'm sure it's doing you good to talk about it to an outsider.'

'Yes, it is,' said Robbie; though he found himself thinking that 'outsider' was not at all an appropriate word. It was more like talking to an old friend.

'Good,' said Paul. 'So pour me some coffee and help yourself to more orange juice, and tell me again about your father's plans for the island.'

* * *

Sarah emerged from the dining room with Jean, closely followed by Brian and Muriel. They all hesitated outside the door, and Sarah made a move towards the main staircase.

'I'd better get back to Paul and see if he needs anything.'

Jean and Brian exchanged glances, but it was Muriel who spoke.

'Nonsense! He's perfectly able to eat his breakfast without you for once. Give the poor man some peace and quiet!'

She turned to Brian and gave his arm a squeeze, and beamed at Jean.

'And that applies to you two, as well. I'm going up to my room now, and you can forget about me and do whatever you like for the rest of the morning. I shall be quite all right; I'm sure I can find plenty of ways to amuse myself.'

'That's just what I'm afraid of!' muttered Brian under his breath to Jean. Muriel swung round and glared at him.

'I heard that! I may be a bit forgetful at times, but I'm not deaf. You mind your manners!'

'Sorry, Mu,' said Brian, giving her an affectionate smile. 'You go ahead and do whatever you feel like doing. We'll probably be somewhere around the hotel or the garden if you need us. We'll meet up again for lunch, shall we?'

'That would be nice, dear,' said Muriel, mollified, and she started up the stairs. Half-way up she turned to deliver her exit-line.

'Though I really don't know why you should think I might need you!'

Jean tucked her arm through Sarah's and led her firmly towards the front door.

'She's quite right, you know. We fuss over them far too much. Come out and walk round the garden with us – Paul will be perfectly all right without you for a while. I'm sure you could do with some fresh air. You look really pale.'

It was more than just pallor; Sarah's skin had the slightly greyish tinge, with dark circles under the eyes, that spoke of stress and exhaustion. She frowned and hesitated, then shrugged and allowed herself to be led out into the garden.

'There you are, you see,' said Jean, looking up at Paul's balcony as they walked away from the building towards the main garden, 'I told you he'd be fine – he's found himself a companion already. He seems to have struck up quite a friendship with young Robbie. Such a nice lad. I'm sure it will do Paul a lot of good to have some younger company.'

'He's certainly looking much better this morning,' said Brian, falling into step beside them as they crossed the lawn.

'He had a better night last night,' admitted Sarah. 'It's the nightmares and panic attacks that leave him so exhausted. They were getting less frequent as he recovered from his operation, but now they've come back again, with all this.'

'That's hardly surprising,' said Brian. 'But it must put a dreadful strain on you, coping with everything alone. Why don't you let us help? I'm sure we could manage to keep an eye on Paul; give you a break sometimes.'

'That's very kind of you. Thank you. We did have a nurse for him when he first came out of hospital, and that made a lot of difference. But as he got better, there didn't seem so much need for her. And anyway, Richard said …' Her voice trembled and she fell silent.

Brian opened his mouth to ask a question, but Jean caught his eye and shook her head, and he thought better of it. They reached a spot in the garden where there was a seat, set by a gap in the shrubs to give a view down to the sea. The sun was beginning its climb up a cloudless sky, and they sat for a while enjoying its warmth. At last Brian spoke again.

'Look, Sarah – I know it's none of my business really, but I think perhaps you should try to get some help for Paul. From what I've seen of him, I don't think he's suffering from the beginnings of senile dementia, like Muriel.'

To his surprise, Sarah responded positively, with more liveliness than he had seen in her since before Richard's death.

'Do you really think so? I've thought that myself, too, especially recently. Seeing Muriel has reminded me of just what it was like with my own mother – and Paul *isn't* the same, not really. I could never get Richard to talk about it, but perhaps now ...'

Once again the sentence trailed off into silence, and the animation faded from her face. When she continued, her voice was flat and lifeless.

'I can't think about anything else until after the inquest and the funeral. They haven't even told me yet when the inquest will be, or given me any idea when the body will be released for burial, so I can't make any arrangements.'

Jean gave Sarah's hand a sympathetic squeeze.

'Just let us know as soon as there's anything we can do to help.'

Brian stood up and leaned forward to look down towards the harbour.

'That could be very soon – there's a group of policemen coming up the path now.'

* * *

Halfway through the morning, Inspector Le Sauvage found himself sympathising with Ted Harris – Neville Blythe was proving difficult to interview. Not difficult in the sense of unco-operative; he was impeccably patient and courteous. It was just that the whole process of questioning him was infuriatingly unproductive. He was a born politician; trying to get any definite statement from him was like picking up quicksilver wearing boxing gloves.

The overall impression he gave was of a concerned bystander, sympathetically aware of events but not directly involved in them; a holiday acquaintance of the Taylors but sadly unable to shed any light on Richard's movements. Either it was all perfectly true, or it was very cleverly done.

Only once, at the very end of the interview, was there even the slightest hint of a crack in the smooth armour. Le Sauvage had brought the questioning to a close and was re-arranging the papers on the table in front of him, and Neville stood to leave, flashing a smile with just the right amount of charm at the WDC who was taking notes. The Inspector looked up briefly with a final question.

'By the way, sir – do you have a boat?'

'Yes, I do, Inspector. It's moored in St Peterport harbour. I haven't actually used it since I arrived on Longuey.'

The answer had come smoothly enough, without a hint of hesitation, but the Inspector was watching closely, and had seen the tell-tale twitching of the muscles at the side of the mouth. He didn't know how many other lies were embedded in the story of non-involvement he had been carefully fed, but he was sure this last answer, at least, would turn out not to be strictly true.

* * *

The next interview, with Muriel, was difficult for completely different reasons. Muriel was eager to be helpful, and the Inspector was sure there was no hint of deception in any of her answers. Unfortunately, there was no need for her to try to obscure the truth – it was obscured effectively enough by her own shaky grasp of reality. As the interview progressed, Le Sauvage became aware that what he was hearing was a hopeless tangle of past and present; fact and fantasy. There were times when he wondered if Muriel even knew who Richard Taylor was. Certainly if the investigation ever came up with a suspect and a trial there would be no way anything Muriel said could be used in court; she could never be produced and cross-examined as a witness. He looked across at the WDC with an agonised expression, and she paused briefly in her note-taking to flash him a smile of sympathy.

'Of course,' said Muriel brightly, 'it was a long time ago. But I never forget a face. It may take me a long time to place it, but I get there in the end, you know.'

'Yes, I'm sure you do,' murmured the Inspector absent-mindedly, wondering if the offer of a cup of tea would make things better or worse. On the whole he thought it wouldn't be wise – it would probably only prolong the agony, and what he really wanted to do was to bring this interview to a close as quickly as possible. He wrenched his attention back to Muriel, who was prattling happily on.

'So of course, when I heard about this dreadful thing that's happened, I wondered immediately if it had anything to do with it. Well, it must have, really, mustn't it? You need to know all about things like that, I'm sure. In case it all connects, like a jigsaw puzzle. I used to be very good at those when I was younger, but my eyesight's not really good enough these days. Such a nuisance, because of the knitting.'

The Inspector sighed and tried to home in on something tangible.

'I'm sorry, Mrs Wilson – can you tell me just who it was that you think you recognised?'

'Richard Taylor, of course,' said Muriel, in the same tone of voice she had used in earlier years when a member of her Sunday School class had been particularly obtuse. 'Really, Inspector, I've told you already. You can check if you like with the young lady over there with the nice smile – I'm sure she's got it all written down.'

'All the same, if we could go through it again – just to make certain I've got it right,' said Le Sauvage craftily.

'Oh, very well. I saw Richard Taylor one day when my son-in-law had taken me to the beach – you'll have to check with him which day it was, but I think it was the day you're asking about. I'd met the Taylors before in the hotel, of course, but it was only after I saw Richard on the beach that I remembered where I'd seen him before. Here, on the island. It must have been the last time I was here.'

'You mean when Mr and Mrs Taylor were here last year? But I thought your daughter told us this was the first time you'd been here on holiday.'

'Oh yes,' said Muriel firmly. The Inspector waited for further clarification but none was forthcoming.

'Do you mean yes, it was last year, or yes, this is your first visit?'

'Oh no, I don't think so. It can't have been, can it? Because I wasn't here then, was I? But I was before, you see, so it all fits in, after all. Like the one that Jean was doing in the lounge.'

'I'm sorry; I don't think I quite follow ...'

'The jigsaw, of course. Really, Inspector, you don't seem to be concentrating at all. You should, you know, because it might turn out to be important, mightn't it; knowing that Richard and I had met before?'

'Ah yes, so it might,' said Le Sauvage, trying to sound as if he knew exactly what she was getting at. 'So it would be helpful if you could remember exactly when this was.'

'Of course I can!' said Muriel triumphantly, 'I'm hardly likely to forget that, am I? I may get a little confused about dates sometimes, but I do remember my own honeymoon! It was a summer very like this one – July 1948!'

# INTERLUDE : JULY 1944

The sun burned away the last curling wisps of cloud, and Hugo could feel the heat building up on his closed eyelids. Drifting contentedly towards sleep, he heard Annette's voice and the joyous barking of the dog from the water's edge as if they were very far away; but the sound of the breaking waves seemed to be coming from somewhere inside his own head. His breathing began to slow, and the sounds of Annette and the dog gradually faded even further into the distance.

The sharp cry of a gull wheeling overhead snapped him back to full consciousness, and he raised himself on one elbow to look out across the broad sweep of the beach.

Already a heat haze shimmered at the edge of the water, and through it he saw Annette's slim figure poised to throw a stick, and the dog looking eagerly up at her.

Further up the beach, in foamy frills left behind by each successive high tide, shells lay thickly scattered; pale pink and white and yellow, broken and whole, common and rare, flung together in heaps or strung out in thin lines.

The dry sand above, soaking up the sun until it almost burned the skin at first touch, was composed almost entirely of fragments of shell, giving the whole beach a slight pearly sheen. Hugo lifted his hand and let the tiny translucent particles pour through his fingers, and they flashed and glittered in the sunlight, pale and beautiful; like Annette.

He lay back on the sand in the little sheltered suntrap between the dunes, and closed his eyes again. Before he had time to drift back towards sleep, he heard the panting of the dog and felt a shadow above him blocking out the heat. He opened his eyes to look up at the dark silhouette leaning over him, and heard her soft voice.

'Look, Hugo. Isn't it beautiful!'

She had found a complete scallop shell, deep coral pink and almost perfectly symmetrical. It lay in her upturned palm, and her slender fingers turned it over to show him the smoothness of the inside.

He reached out lazily to pull her down beside him, and she knelt for a moment laughing down at him. Then she leaned forward to place the shell carefully in the pocket of his jacket, flung down on the sand beside him, before bending her lips to his.

# CHAPTER 12

The incident room in St Peterport was humming with activity as phone calls came through in response to the radio and TV appeals. Many of them were clearly useless; as well as the usual quota of calls from cranks who responded to any appeal, it was amazing how many people rang to report a trip to Longuey which turned out to be for the wrong day. But all calls had to be logged and reported, and gradually the great haystack of information began to build up within which the needles of vital fact would eventually be found.

Late in the morning, Sergeant Harris finished a stint manning a telephone and went in search of a cup of tea. Halfway down the stairs he met Constable Brouard coming up.

'Oh good, I was hoping to find you, sir. There's a couple just arrived in the front office downstairs – I think you might be interested in what they've brought with them.'

'More interesting than a cup of tea, is it?'

Brouard looked disappointed, and Harris took pity on him.

'All right, lad. Wheel them into an interview room and I'll

see what they've got for us. But then you can go and fetch us all some tea before you settle down with that notebook of yours.'

The constable turned and headed back down the stairs, then looked back over his shoulder with an innocent expression.

'Do you want me to pinch some of the custard creams from the Inspectors' room, sir?'

'Is the Pope Catholic?'

'Right you are then. I'll see what I can find.'

Brouard grinned and clattered on down the stairs, and Harris muttered under his breath as he lumbered after him, 'Cheeky young monkey!'

* * *

Mr and Mrs Gibbs couldn't have been more different from one another if they'd dedicated their lives to the attempt. Sergeant Harris found himself remembering a page in the book of nursery rhymes he'd had as a child; the one with a picture of Jack Sprat and his wife. This couple was the other way round, though; the husband short and stout and the wife tall and thin. In addition, Mr Gibbs was dark but balding, red-faced, pompous and loud, where his wife was fair but greying, deathly pale, self-effacing and silent.

Harris munched a custard cream and listened patiently as the husband expounded at length on the duty of all responsible citizens to play their part in the fight against crime, and his own realisation that he had an important contribution to make to the investigation. Inwardly, Harris was seething, but he was a shrewd judge of character and he knew interruption would be futile; might as well try stopping a Mormon in mid-flow on the doorstep. So he avoided catching the constable's eye, and waited for the end of the deluge. Out of the corner of his eye he caught the furious scribbling of Brouard's pen, and he took some comfort from the thought that at least he didn't have to write all this crap down. Let the lad get on with it – serve him right for getting too enthusiastic.

At last there was a gap in the relentless flow, and Harris leapt into it.

'So you were definitely on Longuey with your family on the day in question, sir?'

'Yes indeed, Sergeant. So when we heard the broadcast on the radio, I knew at once that it was my duty as a responsible citizen …'

Harris sighed and took another biscuit. He found himself wondering, not for the first time, why he never seemed to get the witnesses who just came in, made a useful statement and went away again. There must be something about him that attracted all the ones who waffled, ranted or pontificated – and then repeated themselves into the bargain. He waited patiently until the record finally ran down, and then tried again.

'I understand you've brought in some photographs taken on that occasion, sir, and you think they might have some relevance to our enquiries.'

This time he did catch Brouard's eye, and noted the slightly raised eyebrow. Dammit, this pomposity was catching – it had him sounding like a news bulletin himself, now. He leaned forward and nodded encouragingly as Mr Gibbs reached into the bag he had brought with him and took out two packets of photographs.

'That does look quite promising, sir, if they were all taken that day. Something may turn out to be useful, with a bit of luck.'

Mr Gibbs was rummaging in the bag again.

'Oh, it's even better than that, Sergeant,' he said triumphantly. 'Those are just the prints; just wait until you see the slides!'

* * *

Half an hour later, Harris was definitely flagging. He thought wearily that he hadn't been so bored since he'd sat through his brother-in-law's holiday video of a wet camping trip in the Algarve.

The constable had abandoned his notes to join in the attempt to sort the prints and slides into chronological order, hindered rather than helped by a running commentary from Mr Gibbs.

'You have to be sensitive to the possibilities, you see – choose the right equipment for each situation. That's why I always take two cameras with me, and a variety of lenses. Of course, that means when the films are processed, you lose the continuity rather.'

Harris thought that continuity wasn't the only thing that had been lost – spontaneity and interest were other words that sprang to mind. He wouldn't mind betting that Mr Gibbs was the sort of photographer who fussed around for so long setting up a shot that the original elements of the picture had changed or disappeared by the time he actually took it. He continued to examine each print and slide conscientiously, but the hope of finding a shot that included Richard Taylor, or anything else of interest, was fading fast. Hardly any of the photographs had people in them at all, and most of those were of various groupings of the Gibbs family. He stole a glance at Mrs Gibbs, who sat patiently clutching her handbag, making no contribution to the proceedings, and then looked back at the photographs. One of the few things they *had* managed to capture faithfully was her long-suffering expression. He sighed and held the next slide up to the light to squint at it, while Mr Gibbs continued to explain the finer points of aperture settings and depth of field to the constable.

When they finally reached the end, Brouard helped Mr Gibbs to collect up all the photographs and return them to their various containers. He reached for the canvas bag they came in, intending to help pack them away, but was stopped by Mr Gibbs's surprised interjection.

'Surely you need to keep them?'

Harris swept into placatory mode.

'Not just at the moment, sir, thank you. We know where to contact you if necessary, of course, and we're very grateful to you for taking the time to bring them in and show us. But I'm afraid they're of no direct relevance to our enquiries as they stand at present.'

He was quite proud of his self-control; letting the idiot down gently, instead of laying into him for wasting police time, which was what he felt like doing. To his surprise, he saw that Mrs Gibbs was suddenly showing signs of life, standing up and swinging her leather handbag off her shoulder and on to the table. She shot a look of triumph at her husband as she produced from its depths a single pack of photographs and deposited them in front of the Sergeant. Then, for the first time since her murmured greeting when they'd first come in to the room, she spoke.

'Are these any use, Sergeant? My camera's only an Instamatic, I'm afraid, and I'm nothing like the expert my husband is, but I think you'll find some of them have come out rather well.'

* * *

In the end, they did keep all the photographs, as much as anything else to prevent Mr Gibbs losing his temper completely with his wife. Harris wrote out a receipt, thanked them once again for coming in to the station, and nodded to the constable to show them out.

When he had taken Mr and Mrs Gibbs downstairs and finally ushered them off the premises, Brouard came back into the interview room to find Harris still staring intently at one of the photographs.

'Anything useful, sir, or were you just being diplomatic? I thought they were all a bit of a disappointment, myself, for all his high opinion of himself.'

'Oh yes, all his arty crafty stuff is a load of rubbish. All fancy lenses and filters and soft focus and odd angles – you can't make out anything useful from any of 'em. He's not even any good at it. I could've got better effects myself with my old box Brownie.'

'Your what, sir?'

'Never mind, lad. A bit before your time.'

Brouard reached tentatively for the last custard cream, but Harris beat him to it.

'Oh well, not to worry, sir. Can't win 'em all.'

'No,' agreed Harris, licking his finger and mopping up the remaining biscuit crumbs from the plate, 'but you can win some of them. Come and look at this.'

'I thought you said they were all useless?'

'His are. This is one of hers, though. Different kettle of fish altogether, they are. Thank God for idiot-proof cameras with automatic focus. Not that she is an idiot, actually. She's not got a bad eye for composition at all. A bit conventional, maybe, but that's all to the good as far as we're concerned. Fortunately, you see, most people find nice picturesque shots of boats in harbours irresistible, and our friend Mrs Gibbs, bless her, is no exception.'

Brouard leaned over Harris's shoulder and examined the photograph.

'I see what you mean – nice clear picture of all the boats moored in the harbour. So you can tie that up with the list you got from Martel, can't you?'

Harris nodded approvingly.

'Got it in one. But I don't need to check – I can see what I'm interested in right now. Martel gave me the full details of all the boats on his list, and I'm sure there was nothing the size of the biggest one in this photograph. Regular floating gin palace, that is; Martel's list didn't mention anything nearly that classy.'

'So that means either Martel didn't know it was there …'

'Hardly likely. It's big enough, and bang in the middle of the harbour. You'd need to be blind, or stupid, and Martel's not either.'

'… or he left it off the list by accident …'

'Possible, I suppose. He's had a lot on his mind, and I did call him out of the blue. But he's not incompetent, and he keeps regular records of all boats moored at the island.'

'… or he's deliberately lied to us.'

'Exactly. Now I wonder who might have leaned on him to get him to do that – any ideas, constable?'

'I think I can make a fairly good guess, sir.'

Harris nodded thoughtfully.

'You and me both, lad. It doesn't take much in the way of intuition to spot someone in this case who's got the money for a boat like that *and* a strong motive for wanting to avoid publicity.'

'It's not entirely down to intuition, sir. I wouldn't mind betting the boat itself gives us a pretty strong indication.

You're right about how good the automatic focus is on that camera – you can read the name of the boat quite clearly, look.'

'I know – I'd just made that out when you came in. My eyes may not be quite as sharp as yours, but I get there in the end, once I've found my glasses. But how do you make out that the name's significant? "Spirit", it says – lots of boats called "Spirit", I would have thought. Not exactly an original idea.'

'No sir, but it's not usually just "Spirit" by itself. More likely to be "Spirit of" something. "Spirit of the Islands", "Spirit of St Louis", "Spirit of Freedom", – that kind of thing. This one's definitely just the one word; you can see the space before and after it quite clearly in the photo.'

'Well, all right, but what of it?'

'I think the owner's being subtle, sir – showing off without actually drawing attention to himself. I bet you anything you like it's a sort of pun.'

'All right, I give in. For heaven's sake, just come out with it and explain yourself.'

'*Blithe* Spirit, sir. It's Neville Blythe's boat – got to be, hasn't it?. We can check on it, of course, but I'd put money on it right now this minute.'

There was a brief silence while Harris thought about it, then a broad grin spread over his face.

'By Jove, I think he's got it! I would never have thought of that, myself, but you're quite right – it's exactly the sort of clever-dick thing Neville Blythe would do. Well done! You're not just a pretty face, are you, lad? We'll make a detective out of you yet.'

'Thank you very much, sir. Only ...' The constable dropped his eyes and his voice trailed off into indecision.

'Only what, lad?'

Brouard flushed but continued with rash determination,

'Only, do you think you could manage not to call me "lad" all the time? After all, I did stop calling you "Sarge" when you said it was driving you mad. And I'd much prefer "Jim", if you don't mind.'

For a moment there was an ominous silence, and Brouard wondered if he'd misjudged either the man or the moment. Then Harris put his head back and roared with laughter. When he recovered slightly, he spoke surprisingly gently through the remaining rumbles of amusement.

'Right you are, Jim. I'm sorry if I've been irritating you – I wasn't aware I was doing it. I'll do my best to catch myself at it from now on. But you'll have to put up with any lapses, I'm afraid. And of course, you know there's a real problem now with what I might end up calling you.'

'Sorry, sir?'

'Ar-hargh, Jim lad!' said Harris, in a very passable imitation of Robert Newton as Long John Silver, and this time they both laughed together.

# CHAPTER 13

Muriel was having one of her better days. Unfortunately for Jean and Brian, her better days were the ones which were most wearing and difficult to deal with. When the blanket of confusion and dementia really closed in around her, she usually succumbed quite quickly to physical exhaustion, and would spend hours in an armchair, her fingers occupied with one of her pieces of shapeless knitting and her lips moving in soundless muttering.

Today she was bright and chirpy and full of energy, and she came to join them at the breakfast table, waving cheerily to each of the other tables she passed on her way through the dining room. Brian rose to greet her, and gave her a hug before settling her in a chair facing the window.

'Morning, Mu. I can see you had a good night. You look fighting fit this morning.'

'Fit as a flea,' she agreed, carefully pouring orange juice over her cornflakes and tucking in with evident enjoyment. 'These are good,' she said with approval, 'You know, I haven't enjoyed cornflakes so much since I had a craving for them when I was carrying Jean. But then, everything always tastes better on holiday, doesn't it?'

'But Mum, you've put orange juice on them,' said Jean, amused.

'Of course, dear. Doesn't everybody?'

'Of course they do,' agreed Brian, solemnly adding orange juice to his own Weetabix and trying a spoonful. Muriel put down her spoon and looked at him in amazement.

'Brian, what on earth do you think you're doing? Orange juice on Weetabix – are you quite mad?'

'Sorry, Mu,' said Brian meekly, and Jean stifled a giggle.

'Behave yourselves, you two,' she said sternly, 'and let's decide what we want to do today. It looks as if the weather's going to hold, so how about a boat trip while the sea's calm? Do you fancy taking the boat to Sark, Mum?'

'Oh no, dear. I thought I'd go over to Guernsey on the ferry today, with the others.'

'What others?' asked Jean, flashing a worried look at Brian.

'I expect that nice policeman will be there, don't you? Not the young one, the older, tubby one. I liked him; he had kind eyes. And young Robbie, of course, and Sarah and Paul. I don't know who else will be there, but you needn't worry about me. I shall be perfectly all right. Tom will look after me.'

Tom was Jean's elder brother, who had emigrated to New Zealand fifteen years ago. Muriel sailed on, oblivious to the glances being exchanged beside her.

'So you see, I couldn't possibly go to Sark. Not today. I must go to pay my respects, after all, for old times sake. Paul will expect it.'

Brian leaned across the table and took Muriel's hand.

'I think you've been misled, Mu,' he said gently. 'Paul isn't going anywhere today. He's not been well, you know.'

Muriel looked puzzled.

'Are you sure?'

'Positive. You'd do much better to come to Sark with us. Paul won't mind, really.'

She hesitated, then suddenly beamed at him.

'All right then, dear, if you're really sure it's all right. It is odd, though, don't you think? Still, I expect Jean-Pierre just got it wrong.' She leaned forward towards Brian and continued in a loud whisper, 'You know, I don't think he's altogether reliable sometimes. He must have told me the wrong day.'

'The wrong day?'

'For the inquest, of course.'

* * *

The Magistrate's court on Guernsey where the inquest was to be held was small and rather cramped, and seemed cold and dark in contrast to the sunshine outside. Robbie had been told that he didn't actually have to appear as a witness, as the Magistrate who was acting as the Coroner had agreed to accept his written statement about the discovery of the body. At first he had felt slightly indignant, robbed of his moment of importance as chief witness, but now that he was actually sitting in the courtroom he found he was glad he wouldn't have to say anything, after all. He was glad, too, that Claire had come with him, as she served as a buffer between him and Sarah, who was grim-faced and silent and rather intimidating.

He was surprised at how few other people were there; the same two policemen who had interviewed him, plus one other who he thought must be an Inspector, one court official, one man with a briefcase who seemed to represent an

Insurance Company, two journalists in the Press seats, and three other members of the public, none of whom he recognised.

The atmosphere as they waited for the Coroner was hushed but not unfriendly, and there was a low murmur of conversation from the police and the press. Robbie nudged his mother and indicated the three people sitting in the far corner of the room.

'Who do you think they are?' he whispered.

'I don't know. The Court Officer told me there's another inquest immediately after this one, so perhaps they're just here because they're early for that. I don't think this will take long. I can't really think why you wanted to come.'

He didn't know himself, or not in terms of anything she would understand; the nagging feeling that this was *his* body because he'd been the one to find it, the desire to tell Hal he'd been to an inquest – what most of it boiled down to in the end, he supposed, was simple inquisitiveness.

There was something else, too – the need for some sort of recognition of the importance of the death itself. He was unaccountably disappointed so far; he didn't know quite what he had expected, but it certainly hadn't been this matter-of-fact, almost humdrum occasion. When the Magistrate began the proceedings, the sense of disappointment continued; his voice, probably deliberately, was flat and expressionless, carefully and clearly enunciating the details of a man's death as if it were a chapter in a dusty textbook, of no possible interest to anyone but an ancient historian. Robbie listened to that dry voice reading out his own statement about finding the body, and he wanted to stand up and cry out, 'No! It wasn't like that at all. It was terrible and frightening and sad, and you're making it all sound ordinary and unimportant!' He felt somehow cheated and ignored, and began to wish he hadn't come.

* * *

Inspector Le Sauvage was eyeing the Press seats with a certain amount of satisfaction; only one junior hack from the local paper, and a stringer for the nationals. None of the big guns had turned up, so no whiff of anything unusual had got out yet, thank God. He'd done his best with the Presiding Officer, but the Magistrate was a dry old stick and didn't take kindly to being told what was required of him; he'd certainly raised an eyebrow at the suggestion that perhaps the full post-mortem report didn't need to be read out until the resumption. So, it all depended on how much the Press boys picked up from it at this stage. The local lad looked dopey enough; wet behind the ears and bored stiff with the endless round of bread-and-butter reporting. The stringer was a different kettle of fish, though; older, more experienced, and used to relying on his nose for anything which might tickle the fancy of the tabloids.

The Inspector was grateful for the tedium of the Magistrate's delivery that Robbie found so disturbing; perhaps it would lull the gentlemen of the press into inattention for once. Not that he actually approved of any attempt to suppress the full and free availability of information to the public, but he knew just how much harm too much media attention could do to the progress of an investigation, once it was unleashed. His job as investigating officer was going to be difficult enough, without the added stress of pressure from above *and* hounding from the press.

* * *

Sergeant Harris allowed his attention to drift away from the evidence of identification, and his eyes in sweeping round the courtroom settled briefly on the little group of people waiting patiently for the following inquest. He frowned, and leaned forward to get a better view. Surely there had only been three people sitting in that far corner before the inquest began? Now there were four. The fourth person must have slipped in unnoticed at the side of the court as everyone stood for the entrance of the coroner. She – he was almost certain it was a woman – now sat immediately behind the other three, and he needed to shift his position slightly to see her more clearly.

It was subtly done; a scarf over her hair and her eyes hidden by dark glasses, that was all. Not enough of an effort made at disguise to defeat the object of the exercise and make her conspicuous. But it was enough; if he hadn't had her pointed out to him so recently, he wouldn't have recognised her. He looked across at the journalists, and noted with amusement that the spotty youth was proving totally unsuccessful in his attempts to stifle a yawn, and absent-mindedly twiddling a pencil round and round in his fingers. The older man was dividing his attention between his notebook and a section of a tightly folded newspaper; from where he sat, Harris couldn't make out whether it was the Times crossword or Sun bingo. He hoped, for Le Sauvage's sake, that whichever it was would prove enough of a distraction for the journalist not to notice the presence under his very nose of Abigail Meredith, daughter of the Home Secretary, ex-companion of junior Royalty, and current mistress of a likely future member of the Cabinet.

He nudged Constable Brouard, who had just returned to his seat after reading his statement on the identification of the body, and inclined his head towards the little group of people in the far corner of the courtroom. Brouard followed the direction of his glance, and almost immediately nodded in recognition. Harris tore a page from the back of his notebook, wrote on it, 'living dangerously?' and passed it over. The constable added a line underneath and passed it back. Harris read, 'from what I hear, living dangerously is what the lady's good at!' and grinned. He screwed up the paper and put it in his pocket. No sense in alerting the Inspector at this stage; the poor sod probably had enough to worry about already.

* * *

The Pathologist's full post-mortem report provoked a flurry of shorthand from the press. Inspector Le Sauvage was disappointed; he'd hoped that the complexity of the medical language, coupled with the normal reluctance of any pathologist ever to commit himself to a definite conclusion, might have been enough to throw the journalists off the scent. But he always knew it was a forlorn hope; even the inexperienced local boy could hardly miss the implications of the details recounted now with such maddening clarity by the Magistrate. The unusual bruising and injuries to the ribs, and the small quantity of water present in the lungs, might not in themselves have been enough to ring alarm bells, but what made even the spotty youth sit up and take notice was the description of the marks on the face and shoulders.

When the Coroner announced that he was adjourning the inquest at the request of the Police, to allow them time to make further enquiries, the local journalist remained in the courtroom to cover the next inquest, but the stringer, no doubt already deciding which editor to approach first, rushed out to find a phone.

The Inspector reflected ruefully that Longuey would soon be besieged by tabloid journalists, and he had little doubt that they would begin by homing in on the hotel registers. He sighed heavily, and began composing in his mind various possible openings for his next conversation with the Chief Superintendent. Harris had noted the stringer's hurried exit, and savoured the agonised expression it had produced on the Inspector's face. Not for the first time, he thought how fortunate he was never to have been saddled with all the problems which came with promotion.

There was a general shuffling and movement in the court as the Court Officer checked through his papers for the next inquest. Harris looked across the room to the group of people in the far corner.

There were now only three of them.

* * *

On the ferry back to Longuey, Robbie wanted to talk to his mother about the inquest, but he found himself completely intimidated by the presence of Sarah. She was no longer silent, as she had been on the outward journey, but she chatted to Claire with remorseless intensity about the weather, the hotel, Robbie's school; anything but Richard or the inquest. Robbie watched a tiny dribble of saliva form itself at the corner of her mouth as the sentences tumbled after one another with no pause for breath, and listened to the note of hysteria rising in her voice, and he felt embarrassed and a little afraid. He was sure she must be very close to the point of breakdown, and he was ashamed that his overwhelming reaction was not sympathy but a selfish desire for escape. He felt intense relief when at last the ferry docked and Sarah left them and made her way up the steep path to the hotel.

He spent the rest of the day on the other side of the island, but as he swam and sunbathed and walked the paths through the dunes he couldn't get out of his memory the intensity of Sarah's stare, or the catch in her voice as she ran the mindlessly banal sentences together.

* * *

The long day drew finally to a close, and in the hotel the public rooms were silent and empty. The staff had left for their living quarters in the block of flatlets further down the hill, and Bernard had locked his office, done his final rounds and retired to bed. Only in some of the private rooms was there still movement.

* * *

Neville lay face-down on the bed. Abigail , wearing his blue and white striped silk dressing-gown, knelt beside him, her skilful hands busily kneading his tanned skin.

'Your shoulder muscles are simply rigid with tension,' she said with disapproval. 'I've never felt them so knotted up.'

'I'm not surprised,' said Neville lightly. 'It must be the effect you have on my life. There are times when I regret ever having met you. I should have known better – I could see from the very beginning that you were trouble.'

'You know very well that was half the attraction.'

'More than half,' agreed Neville, stretching lazily under her probing fingers. 'I knew I'd found a kindred spirit. Well worth taking risks for. Planned risks, though. This business with Richard is rather more than I'd bargained for.'

'I've been thinking about that,' said Abigail slowly, frowning in concentration. 'I've got some ideas of my own about it, as a matter of fact.'

'What sort of ideas?' asked Neville sharply. 'Keep out of

it, Abby. We've done well to avoid notice so far; I don't want you stirring things up that are better left undisturbed.'

'It depends whether the return would be worth the risk. If I see something that doesn't really register at the time, but it starts to make sense afterwards, I don't see any reason why I shouldn't try to make use of it. After all, why tell the police? That wouldn't help us to go on avoiding notice, would it?'

'Be careful, Abby. There are times when you're just too devious for your own good.'

'I'm not so devious I can't make my meaning clear when I want to. And when I see a way of using an interesting piece of information, I'm always quite open about asking what's in it for me. Don't move! I was just beginning to get somewhere, and you've tensed right up again.'

She worked on in silence until she felt the muscles begin to relax once more, but her busy fingers had done nothing to remove the tension in Neville's voice when he spoke again.

'You're a fool, Abby! Taking risks is one thing, but this is just plain dangerous. It's not a game, you know.'

'Yes it is. Everything's a game. Some games are just more exciting than others, that's all.'

'Don't be childish.'

'I thought you liked me to be childish.'

'For heaven's sake, Abigail ...' began Neville, turning his head to look at her. There was a faint whisper of silk as the blue and white stripes slithered to the floor.

'Mmm,' she said, continuing to knead rhythmically, 'you only ever call me Abigail when you're going to be stuffy. You know I prefer Abby. And since you've accused me of being childish, I might as well teach you a new game.'

'Not now, Abby – I'm not in the mood.'

'All the better for the game I have in mind. Perfect, in fact. Let's play hide-and-seek.'

'What do you mean?' asked Neville, exasperated, but intrigued in spite of himself.

'I'll count and you have to hide. Only it's a variation on hiding. All you have to do is try to ignore me while I count up to ten. Starting now. One.'

'That shouldn't be difficult.'

'You'd be surprised,' she said, shifting her position so that he had an uninterrupted view. 'I'm allowed to do anything I like to distract you. Two.'

Neville watched her in silence for a moment, then said coldly,

'You're really very good, I'll give you that. But I told you, I'm not interested. I have other things on my mind.'

'It's not your mind I'm aiming at. And I can be much more interesting than this. Like this, for instance. Or this. Three.'

'Wasted effort. I don't have to watch you,' said Neville, turning his head away and burying it in the pillow. Abigail laughed softly and leaned over him to whisper in his ear.

'First sign of weakness. Retreat only postpones the final defeat. I do have other strategies, you know. What about this? Four.'

Neville groaned and clenched his fists, and she laughed again.

'Fascinating things, muscles, aren't they?. They take orders from the brain, of course. But they also respond directly to physical stimulus. And there are such a lot of them. In such interesting places. I wonder how many of them the brain can control at once? Five.'

'Damn you, Abby,' muttered Neville, but without much conviction.

'I should think there's a fair chance I'll be damned anyway, without relying on a recommendation from you. We might as well be damned together; why not just relax and enjoy it? That's better. There are distinct possibilities of a further advance, now, I think. Turn over. Six.'

'Christ, Abby! You never learned that at Cambridge'

'Cambridge taught me a lot, actually. Some of it even within the syllabus of my course, you'll be surprised to know. But it didn't teach me this, I agree. I'd learned this long before Cambridge. All Cambridge gave me was plenty of opportunity for keeping my hand in. So to speak. Seven.'

'I hate to admit it, but I think you may be winning this game.'

'It does begin to look extremely likely, doesn't it?'

'Does that mean the counting stops now?'

'Of course not,' she said, her voice muffled, 'It's not that sort of game. Eight.'

'What happens when you get to ten?'

'Don't you know anything about hide-and-seek? The count always ends with the traditional words.'

'What words?'

'Coming, ready or not.'

'Ah,' said Neville, thoughts of danger receding rapidly from the forefront of his attention. 'In that case, I may as well be magnanimous in defeat. How about nine?'

'No hurry,' murmured Abigail, raising her head briefly to flash him a wicked grin, 'there's always eight and a half.'

* * *

Much, much later, they lay back to back in silent darkness; each wrapped in deep and dangerous thought; each thinking the other wrapped in sleep.

# CHAPTER 14

The day after the inquest was flat and rather depressing. Robbie mooned about aimlessly all day, unable to summon up enthusiasm for any one activity but reluctant to settle into idleness for long enough to examine the thoughts that lay in wait for him.

It seemed to him that his mood reached out to envelop everyone he came into contact with, even the hotel guests who knew nothing of Richard's death or the inquest. There was an air of sombre lethargy spread over the entire island like a suffocating blanket; even the day-trippers on the beaches seemed subdued and sluggish. In fact, this had nothing to do with Robbie's state of mind but everything to do with the weather, which was gradually closing in and becoming oppressive. It was not the sultry heaviness that often precedes a thunderstorm, but a clammy dampness building up in the air, eventually manifesting itself in the appearance of a sea-fog. The temperature fell steadily as the humidity increased, and when the first faint haze of mist began to build up over the land it triggered a grumbling exodus from the beaches.

By the time the last ferry of the day pulled away from the harbour in the early evening, the fog had thickened until the outline of Guernsey was faint and almost indistinguishable. There was not enough of a breeze to ruffle the surface of the water, but still the wisps of mist came spinning in off the sea like the first frail fingers of candyfloss reaching out for the stick. As the pale sun sank towards the horizon the mist thickened and gradually blotted it out altogether, and the wisps gathered into clouds steadily rolling in over the land. Soon even the boats anchored in the deep water off the longest beach could no longer be seen from the shore, and the deep note of the foghorn rang out through the damp, chilly air.

Dinner in the hotel was a strangely festive occasion, with most of the guests more than usually animated, as if in compensation for the muffling effect of the atmosphere outside. If there seemed to be a slight edge of hysteria to the brightness of some of the conversation, nobody was willing to draw attention to it.

As the various groups drifted into the lounge for coffee after their meal, much of the talk was of the weather, and the chances of it continuing the next day. If it didn't clear overnight, the fog would be far more effective than rough weather in stopping the ferries from getting through. Several families who had intended to go across to Guernsey for the day were revising their plans, and there was much speculation about whether it would still be possible to run the boat trip round the island that was planned for the next morning.

Robbie sat curled up in an armchair, in the corner of the lounge furthest from the dining room. He'd eaten his own meal much earlier, in the kitchen with Jean-Pierre. He'd offered to help with the preparation of the salads for dinner, which he'd often done before when the kitchen was busy, but the offer had been declined; there were no evening groups from the mainland tonight because of the fog, so the dining room was comparatively sparsely occupied. Robbie could see Jean-Pierre's point, but he was disappointed. He had no wish to embarrass the kitchen staff by encroaching on their territory uninvited, but the activity would have been welcome as an antidote to the day's uneasy lethargy. He was half inclined to go straight back to the cottage, but he knew Claire wanted time to work undisturbed on the documents she had brought back from her visit to Edward, so he was reluctant to arrive back too early. Instead, he settled himself in the lounge with the same book he had been trying, unsuccessfully, to read for what was beginning to feel like weeks now, not days. When his concentration lapsed, which it did frequently, he switched his attention to the other occupants of the lounge.

From the small alcove quite near him came the low murmur of conversation in French. Robbie had noticed the couple sitting there before; a short, stout, balding and rather pompous Frenchman who Bernard said was a publisher, and his companion. From where he sat, Robbie could only see the companion. He tried not to stare, but it was difficult; she was really quite spectacular. When he had first seen her, glimpsed from a distance, he had immediately labelled her 'dolly bird'. It was only when he saw her at closer quarters that he realised how incongruous that description was. She must be getting on for forty, but she dressed like a rather tarty teenager. Tonight she wore a scarlet flounced mini-skirt, a low-cut black top, black tights and white high-heeled strappy sandals. Her hair was scraped back into a pony-tail held in place by a white butterfly clip, and the huge white beads of her necklace were surpassed in size by her not-quite-matching earrings.

The sharp-featured little face was not unattractive, with a good complexion and a natural tan, but marred by garish blue eye-shadow and a miserable expression. Examining her surreptitiously from behind the pages of his book, Robbie thought that she would really have done better to avoid exposing her knees and elbows, which were bony and ugly and definitely not young.

It seemed that the Frenchman had no such reservations about her knees, one of which he was caressing determinedly with the plump hand which was all Robbie could see of him. There was no mistaking the tone of desire in his low murmuring voice; clearly he was besotted with her. Even more clearly, this did not make her wildly happy.

Robbie transferred his attention to the other couple deep in private conversation, in the alcove on the other side of the fireplace. Abigail too was wearing black and red, but the fact only underlined the difference between her and the rather pathetic creature sitting so close to her. Abigail's silk shirt was crimson rather than scarlet, worn over a long black skirt slit to the knee, and her hair was loosely tied back with a matching crimson ribbon. She had the careless grace born of youth and supreme self-confidence, and her face glowed with vitality. But there was something in the set of her mouth that Robbie found disturbing; a cruelty in her smile that made him shudder. As he looked from one side of the fireplace to the other he found himself thinking, to his own surprise, that he much preferred the older woman's face.

The other spaces in the lounge were all occupied by groups, either families or gatherings of friends and holiday acquaintances. Most of the children present were involved, as players or spectators, in a fairly raucous game of Monopoly, which Robbie had politely declined to join in. He had looked in vain for Paul when he first came into the room; neither

Sarah nor Paul seemed to have come down to dinner, and he thought they would probably have had their meal in Paul's room rather than facing other people in the dining room.

Brian and Jean Wilson were part of a large group seated round the low table by the main window, but Robbie was amused to see that Muriel had drifted across to join the children; she was perched on the arm of a chair and totally absorbed in the progress of the game. He had decided he liked Muriel. Her conversation was decidedly strange most of the time, but it often made a sort of surreal sense that appealed to his sense of humour, and she was always friendly and cheerful.

He returned to his book for a while, until a particularly loud burst of laughter from the Monopoly players made him look up again. He glanced around the room and noticed that Abigail was no longer in her chair but on her way to the door. He watched as Neville lingered briefly over his brandy, then casually put down his empty glass and rose to follow her. It was a finely-judged pause; just long enough to establish them as discreetly separate rather than obviously together. In contrast, the stout publisher, who had wined rather too well, was beginning to draw attention to himself. The low murmurings of his voice, thick with desire and alcohol, were increasing in volume as his hand strayed further up the black-clad thigh and began to fumble at the edge of the scarlet skirt. Robbie was not the only person in the room to be relieved when the woman twisted out of the grasp of the searching fingers and abruptly excused herself. As she left the room the man half-rose to follow her, but changed his mind and waved to the wine-waiter to bring him another bottle.

Robbie didn't quite know whether to be amused or sickened by these examples of human relationships in action. He couldn't decide which was worse; the publisher's vulgarity or Neville's sleekness. But he found himself decidedly more cheerful about his own problems. Whatever his father was up to, he didn't think it was likely to be an involvement with another woman.

He felt he needed to get away from the hotel, and the thought struck him that it wasn't too late to try phoning Hal; not from the hotel pay-phone, which wasn't particularly private, but from the harbour phone-box before he went back to the cottage. He knew he didn't have enough change on him, so he went to look for his father.

To Robbie's annoyance, Bernard was nowhere to be found. He could usually be tracked down in his office after dinner, if he wasn't circulating in the lounge or one of the bars. But tonight the office door was locked, and Robbie's quick search through the public rooms was fruitless. As he stood by the front door, wondering where else to try, Abigail came down the main staircase and swept past him and out into the garden. He half expected Neville to appear and follow her, but the staircase and hall remained deserted.

He decided to try the kitchen; if his father wasn't there perhaps he could borrow some money from Jean-Pierre instead. But there was no sign of Jean-Pierre either, and in the end the only person he could find to lend him some change was one of the chambermaids.

* * *

The mist rolling in from the sea continued to thicken as the light faded, until shapes became difficult to distinguish even at close range. The air was thick and damp and startlingly cold, and up on the cliff-top Abigail shivered in spite of her heavy coat. The mournful boom of the fog-horn filtered through the evening air, at regular intervals just long enough to stretch the nerves to breaking point in the wait for the next one. Other, smaller sounds were muffled in the fog and lost, so that Abigail did not hear the footsteps of the person climbing the cliff path until the moment before a dark shape loomed out of the mist towards her and became recognisable.

* * *

Harris, kneeling on the carpet surrounded by papers he had brought home with him, was deeply absorbed in a list of products manufactured by one of Richard Taylor's subsidiary companies when a sharp noise from the kitchen startled him out of his concentration. He tensed, then relaxed immediately when he realised what it was.

'Hello, you bad boy!' he scolded. 'What time do you call this to come swanning home for your tea, then?'

The cat-flap still swung gently to and fro in the kitchen as the living room door was pushed open and a shaggy ginger head appeared, accompanied by a loud purr. The head was followed by a damp and straggly long-haired body, ending in a massively fluffy tail that only needed to be a brighter shade of orange to do duty as the revolving brush in a drive-in car-wash.

The purr advanced determinedly across the carpet and the body sat itself firmly down on the paper Harris was in the middle of reading, the tail obscuring the very section he was about to move on to. He groaned.

'You're a pain, Mycroft – do you know that?'

The purr rumbled on unabated, and Harris sighed.

'Yes, of course you do – you know everything. Like the exact spot to sit on so that I have to stop reading. Why can't you go and drape yourself over the sheets I've finished with, you daft animal?'

The exasperation was only superficial, overlaying a core of indulgent affection. Once, years ago, there had been two fluffy marmalade kittens, and it had been Harris's wife who had named the brothers Sherlock and Mycroft, firmly overruling his own suggestion of Reggie and Ronnie. After Mary's long illness and eventual death, he had submerged himself determinedly in the job, using it as a barricade, refusing to acknowledge or admit his pain, even to himself. It was only six months later, when Sherlock had been run over, that he had cried for the cat as he had been unable to cry for Mary, and in doing so had at last found a release for his grief. Now, he and Mycroft had a lot in common; loners, getting a bit long in the tooth, but still dogged hunters nevertheless.

He stretched out a hand to tickle the cat behind its ears. The purr increased in volume as Mycroft got up off the paper and waved his tail in Harris's face.

'Ugh – you're wet! What have you been up to? It's only mist outside, for heaven's sake – you must have been rolling around in wet grass to get yourself in this state. If you *must* sit on my reports, you need a good cleaning up first. Where's your comb?'

Still on his knees, he twisted round to grope behind the armchair for the spot on the floor where the cat's brush and comb usually ended up.

Mycroft, treating the sudden movement as an invitation to play, leapt on to Harris's shoulder and stuck a cold damp nose into his ear.

Harris, taken by surprise, lost his balance and fell heavily, the hand that had been outstretched behind the armchair taking most of his weight.

'Ow!' he yelled, and rolled over shaking his hand vigorously in the air.

'You daft cat, Mycroft, what did you want to do that for?'

He nursed his right hand in his left armpit until the pain began to subside. Mycroft retreated to a safe distance and watched him with interest to see if the game was going to be repeated. Harris shook his head ruefully.

'My own fault, I suppose. I ought to put your brush and comb away properly each time, not leave them on the floor so that I have to grovel for them. Well – I've found them now, all right – I put my hand down right on the bloody brush.'

He took his hand out of its hiding place to inspect the damage. The brush was a particularly tough one, designed to cope with long-haired cats, and its stiff bristles had left their imprint clearly on the skin of his palm.

Tiny indentations like pinpricks, clustered closely together.

'Well, I'll be damned!' said Harris softly to himself. 'A brush – why the hell didn't we think of that before? That's it! A deck-brush – got to be. The poor bastard was held under with a deck-brush.'

He shuddered at the pictures that were forming in his mind. Richard, a weak swimmer, floundering desperately within sight of the boat but unable to reach it; the brush stretched out as a blessed means of salvation; the frantic grab towards help and safety. And then, the relief changing to horror redoubled; the means of rescue turned into an instrument of death, ruthlessly pushing downwards, holding him under.

Harris was a fairly strong swimmer himself, but that didn't stop him from having a particular morbid fear of drowning. There were times when a vivid imagination, normally an asset to a detective, became a distinct disadvantage; this was one of them.

He found it only too easy to conjure up for himself Richard's despair and panic; an intolerable pressure building relentlessly in the lungs, and all the while a last frenzied scrabbling with weakening fingers at the cruel bristles jabbing downwards, until the final roaring blackness.

Harris shook himself and scrambled to his feet, wrenching his thoughts back towards life and the comfort of pressing domestic detail.

'Come on, Mycroft,' he muttered, 'Let's get you fed before I get too depressed. Serves me right for bringing the job home with me, I suppose.'

He shambled out to the kitchen with Mycroft dancing ecstatically round his ankles. By the time he'd fed and combed the cat and poured himself another beer, he'd lost all desire to wade through any more reports, so he scooped up all the papers and packed everything back into the file. There was a tiny voice at the back of his mind nagging at him to register something that he should have noticed as significant, but he ignored it, determined not to stir up his imagination again.

Even so, when he dozed off in the armchair with a replete Mycroft draped contentedly across his knees, his dreams were full of thrashing limbs and dark swirling water.

* * *

Robbie, standing outside the phone box by the harbour wall waiting to phone Hal, blew on his fingers to warm them up a little before tucking them deep into his pockets. He had come out without a coat, not expecting to have to wait in the cold, clammy air for very long, but the large lady wedged firmly into the phone box seemed to have embarked on the recital of some sort of epic saga, and she had a pile of coins stacked up on the ledge in front of her that looked as if it would last her until Christmas. Robbie doggedly stood his ground, positioning himself so that she could see that he was waiting, and trying to look like someone with a life-or-death call to make. The woman looked at him briefly, then re-manoeuvred her considerable bulk to turn her back on him. He hunched his shoulders and stamped his feet against the cold that was seeping into him, as the damp mist came sweeping steadily in from the sea.

Eventually he was driven into more definite movement to try to keep warm, and he walked the short distance to the harbour wall and then up and down alongside it, keeping a watchful eye on the phone box. The fog was getting much thicker now, and even at this close range objects were disappearing, but the light spilling out from the box made its outline, though blurred, still visible. He listened to the sound of the water lapping against the wall, and the deep note of the foghorn wailing like some huge animal in pain.

Then suddenly there was another sound, fainter and from a different direction, but like an echo of the foghorn at a higher pitch; a terrifying wail that came to an abrupt end.

Robbie shivered, not only from the cold, and strained his ears to see if the sound would be repeated, but there was nothing but the steady lap of the water until the foghorn's next note, and he wondered if he had really heard anything else at all. Then his eye caught the movement of the phone box door as the woman edged out at last and lumbered away, swallowed up almost immediately by the omnivorous fog. With a sigh of relief, Robbie headed towards light and comparative warmth, and the thought of the comfort of hearing Hal's voice pushed the memory of all other sounds from his mind.

* * *

By the time Robbie had finished his conversation with Hal, the dark figure that stumbled down the path from the cliffs had reached the back entrance to the hotel grounds; it stood for a moment to regain its composure, and then slipped silently through the gate and across the back lawn, the fog closing in around it like a cloak of invisibility

# INTERLUDE : MARCH 1945

The evening light poured through the farmhouse window and gave an extra glow to the polished flagstones of the kitchen floor. Annette stood up and cleared the plates away from the long wooden table. Hugo sighed, and stretched in contentment.

'I should go back,' he said, 'It's getting late.' There was no conviction in his voice, and he made no move to get up from the table. Annette came and stood behind him, her fingers resting lightly on his shoulders.

'Come out to the barn,' she said. 'Come and meet the new calf. A heifer this time, but very like the one you helped me with, that first time. Do you remember?'

He reached his hand up to cover hers, and squeezed her fingers gently.

'Of course I remember. How could I ever forget.'

They were silent for a while. He wondered if, like him, she was remembering everything else that had happened since that day; if her memory, like his, was treasuring every tiniest detail. At last he spoke again.

'You managed without me this time.'

'It was easy, this time. I didn't need anyone's help.'

He knew it would be better if he stayed silent, but he couldn't.

'Why does he leave you to cope with so much alone? This is his farm; his responsibility. He shouldn't leave so much of the burden on you all the time. Where is he?'

'He's out,' she said simply, 'That's all you need to know. He's out with the boat and he probably won't be back until late. Isn't that why you're here?'

Hugo nodded. He knew that the expeditions with the boat had to be more than just fishing trips, but for several reasons he was unwilling to investigate further. For anyone with local knowledge and good seamanship, no doubt it was possible – even easy – to reach the other islands undetected. He knew that what he *should* do was to report it to his superiors on Guernsey. He also knew he had no intention of doing that. He tried to tell himself that it was just for Annette's sake, but it was difficult to suppress his shame at the knowledge that a large part of the reason was pure selfishness; these very absences gave him the long uninterrupted stretches of time with her that had become so precious to him.

She took his hand and pulled him to his feet.

'Come,' she said, 'It's warmer in the barn. You needn't worry about Paul – forget about him, and come with me.'

* * *

It was later, when the golden glow had faded from the flagstones, that the door opened and a tall young man in dark trousers and a fisherman's sweater came into the kitchen. Crossing to the sink, he filled a glass from the tap and gulped the water greedily, then stood wiping his hand across his mouth as he stared down at the plates still waiting to be washed.

He moved away from the sink and cut himself a slice of bread and a hunk of cheese, looking slowly round the room as he ate it. Slung carelessly across the back of one of the chairs at the kitchen table was a jacket; the dull grey jacket of a German army uniform. He didn't need to look closely at the badges of rank to know whose it was.

Swallowing the last of the cheese, he picked up the jacket and stood for a long time deep in thought, his strong brown fingers mechanically stroking the rough material. He'd known for some time that the Captain's visits to the farm were far too frequent to be explained merely by a sense of duty to his official responsibilities. He'd never raised the subject with Annette – there were difficulties enough, just surviving this war, without inviting further heartache. There would be time enough later, perhaps, to explore his feelings; better for the moment to remain numb – cold and hard enough to survive whatever was to come.

Meanwhile, here was an opportunity to be turned to his advantage. A German officer's jacket would afford him extra insurance against discovery – might buy him precious time if challenged.

He slipped his arms into the sleeves and hunched the jacket over his shoulders, beginning to button it up as he went outside into the fading light.

# CHAPTER 15

The booming of the foghorn continued through the night and on into the next morning, while the fog over the sea thinned but refused to disperse completely. Dawn broke over the island to reveal a landscape that existed in fitful fragments, as the mist patches broke up and retreated only to reform and drift back.

The dining room was empty of its usual early risers, who had mostly taken the fog as an excuse for an extra lie-in. The first group down for breakfast included most of the people who had booked themselves for the bird-watching trip round the island and its surrounding rocky islets. There was much speculation on the subject of the trip and whether it would be called off because of the weather. When the girl on the reception desk said there had been no message to cancel any arrangements, the little group wound its way rather reluctantly down the steep path to the harbour through the billowing mist, with some grumbling and several expressions of doubt. Most members of the group were surprised to find the boat waiting for them at the harbour steps.

Robbie, who had come from the cottage and reached the

harbour just as the boat was pulling in, was not at all surprised to see it arrive. He'd long ceased to be amazed at the number of times this trip had started out in what looked like being impossible conditions, only for the weather to clear as if by magic once the boat was under way. He gave the skipper a wave, and went to make himself useful, greeting the party from the hotel and helping them aboard.

* * *

The mist swirled and shifted, closing in around the boat and retreating again like a playful puppy clamouring for attention. Sometimes it tired of the game and withdrew altogether, allowing an uninterrupted view of the coastline for minutes at a time. Then it returned to blot out the land again, often with a perverse instinct for masking the position of major bird colonies just as the boat approached them.

Robbie stood beside the skipper in the wheelhouse and listened to the debate that was developing behind them on whether to go on or turn back. The passengers seemed to be evenly divided; the dedicated bird-watchers determined not to lose any opportunity, however slight, of using their binoculars; the less dedicated uncomfortably aware of being cold and damp and unable to see much, and yearning for the hotel lounge and coffee. He caught the skipper's eye and they exchanged grins. They both knew the debate was irrelevant. The boat was chartered and the fee paid. The trip, once started, would continue unless the conditions became actually dangerous. The skipper was a shrewd businessman as well as a good seaman; passengers' discomfort and frustration were not sufficient reasons to merit refunds. In any case, the trip had passed the point where it would take as long to go back, against a strong current, as to continue.

In fact, the grumblings mostly ceased as the boat reached the south-eastern tip of the island and rounded the fort and the islets beyond it. The foghorn had stopped, the mist rolled back to allow a relatively clear view, and there were even glimpses of sun and clear sky. There were plenty of birds to be seen on the rocks and in the sky above them, and bobbing in the water; kittiwakes and oyster-catchers and herring-gulls, sleek black cormorants neatly diving, and terns dive-bombing, folding their wings at the last possible second before entering the water.

By the time the mist closed in again and the boat continued around the northern coastline, even the least avid bird-watchers had ceased to mutter about the trip being a waste of time and money. Although it had returned, the mist was not so thick, and from time to time it allowed glimpses of other bird colonies along the cliffs above the old harbour.

Robbie went forward to the bow-rail as the boat rounded the next rocky outcrop, and lifted his own binoculars to his eyes. The mist had mostly retreated, but still swirled sulkily around the shoreline, parting briefly to reveal the rock formations at the cliff base and then closing them off from sight again. He swept his binoculars over the rocks and the water around them, hoping for a glimpse of a puffin. He knew it was a forlorn hope, although this bay was the home of the main puffin colony; it was too late in the season. By the time the summer term was over each year most of the puffins had already left, and this year he was home a week later than usual because of the scout camp. The best he could hope to see was the odd straggler, perhaps one of this season's young birds that hadn't managed to leave with the others.

He kept sweeping the surface of the water, hoping to catch a glimpse of the distinctive red and yellow beak of a puffin bobbing in the waves, but the mist came swirling in again and he lowered the binoculars in exasperation. At the very moment that he did, his eye caught a movement of red in the water close to the edge of the rocks along the shoreline. He raised the binoculars again and tried to home in on the spot, but the edges of the mist shifted and billowed and made it difficult to judge the position of anything in the water. Then all at once he had it, and he sharpened the focus until he could see what it was: not a red beak at all, but a floating crimson ribbon. He frowned as he tried to remember where he had seen a ribbon like it recently, and then the sun stabbed through the clouds overhead, the mist rolled back like a curtain from the rocks it had been hiding, and he didn't need to wonder any more.

Abigail's coat had fallen open, and her crimson silk shirt had ripped on the sharp edges of the rocks; the delicate material floated and swirled as the waves tugged at it where her crumpled body lay half in, half out of the water at the foot of the cliffs.

Robbie had never been seasick in his life, but now, remembering the terrible wail from last night and its abrupt end, he dropped the binoculars, hung over the rail of the boat and retched until his face was a deathly white and his knees turned to jelly.

# CHAPTER 16

Harris woke with a headache and the niggling feeling that he'd forgotten something vital. This was a not unfamiliar feeling, and generally meant that he *had* forgotten something vital. He knew from previous experience that the only hope of retrieving whatever it was lay in refusing even to try to think about it. It would then almost invariably pop back into his mind some time later with no reason or warning. The frustration was that there was about a 50-50 chance that by then it would be too late to be useful. He tried to empty his mind as much as possible, to create an inviting vacuum for the lost thought to rush back into. The only result of this was that he got halfway to work before he realised he'd left his files at home, and going back for them didn't improve his temper.

In the incident room the information was beginning to mount up, to the point where it was already becoming difficult to see the wood for the trees. Harris chewed at his bottom lip as he sifted through yet another batch of interviews with day-trippers, none of which yielded anything useful. It was hardly likely that they would, really, he thought gloomily; most people who go to the beach for the day put a lot of effort into *not* noticing the other people around them.

More encouraging was the report from the St. Peterport harbour-master. The boat 'Spirit' *was* registered in the name of Neville Blythe, and although it was indeed now moored in the harbour, there was some doubt about exactly when it had arrived. There would have to be more checking, but there was at least a possibility that the boat had still been somewhere around Longuey on the night of Richard's death, and had been transferred to Guernsey during the hours of darkness. The more Harris thought about it, the more convinced he was that Richard had gone into the water from the deck of Neville Blythe's boat. Not quite knowing whether to be pleased or not with this conclusion, he went to tell the Inspector.

Le Sauvage listened silently, then nodded in acquiescence.

'Right, Ted. Time to lean on the right honourable member a little more heavily, I think. If he wants to emerge from this one without any scandal, he'd better stop messing us about and come up with some convincing explanations.'

'It's stretching credulity a little too far for it to be just coincidence, don't you think, sir?' Harris said with some satisfaction. 'We start to suspect that there must have been a boat involved – and his boat just happens to be unaccounted for. There *must* be a connection. And I'll tell you another thing that ties in; I've had an idea what might have caused those marks on the face and shoulders of the body.'

He explained his thoughts about the probable use of some kind of brush, finishing triumphantly, 'I'd put money on it; you'll find something of the sort on Blythe's boat, sir. In my days of pottering about in boats we swabbed the decks with a mop, but you don't get anything like that on big flash boats like Blythe's these days; they all use a high-pressure hose jet and a brush – a brush with really stiff nylon bristles.'

Le Sauvage was clearly impressed, and responded with more enthusiasm than Harris had expected.

'All right – I think you may be on to something there. It gives us something to check, anyway. Get on to the pathologist and ask him if he'd agree those pinpoint abrasions might have been caused by bristles. And find out if there's a brush on Blythe's boat; if so, get it to the lab boys for testing. They can compare the pattern of the marks on the skin with the spacing of the bristles, and see if they can get a match. That could well take care of "How". But does it necessarily lead us directly on to "Who"?'

'It gets us a damn sight closer, sir, surely? If not Blythe himself, then someone who had access to his boat. That has to be a fairly select circle, I would have thought.'

The Inspector frowned.

'Let's not get too far ahead of ourselves. Coincidences do sometimes happen, after all – it *might* have been a different boat altogether. And of course, Blythe's boat may well have been used, with or without his permission, without him being directly involved in what happened on it. But it certainly looks as if he must know *something* he's not telling us.'

'Interview him again today then, sir?'

'The sooner the better. Martel has got some explaining to do, too, though I wouldn't mind betting he was browbeaten into whatever covering up has been going on. If you take Martel and I take Blythe, we can play them off against one another and see if their stories tally.'

'Right you are, sir,' said Harris, moving towards the door. The Inspector called him back.

'Not so fast, Ted. Sit down for a minute, and I'll fill you in on the other information that's come in since yesterday. I think you'll find it interesting. I certainly did.'

Harris pulled up a chair and sat down.

'Something about the money, is it?'

'Indirectly, yes. The money, and the will. More specifically, *two* wills.'

Harris frowned. The Inspector was waiting for him to ask a question, but he took his time, and thought it out for himself.

'Richard's and Paul's.'

Le Sauvage nodded.

'Paul's being much the more interesting. Richard's will is quite straightforward – as far as any will can be straightforward when company finances are involved. There are complicated provisions for the disposal of shares, and the actual running of the company. But the basic provision is that the wife gets a controlling interest in everything. Much as we expected it would be, really – there are no children, and no other close relatives mentioned. No surprises there.'

'But in Paul's will ...?'

'Ah, yes, Paul's will – a surprise there, all right. There's a clause that mentions a second child.'

'Come off it, sir! You don't mean Richard has a long-lost brother?'

'Or sister – the sex isn't actually specified. Yes, Ted, I do mean exactly that. The solicitor who drew up the will wasn't happy about it at the time, but apparently the old man insisted. He gave definite instructions. In the event of Richard's death, every effort is to be made to trace the child, referred to as born to an Annette Taylor.'

Harris whistled.

'A previous marriage! That really puts the cat among the pigeons! What happens to the inheritance then?'

He paused while he thought it through, then shook his head in bewilderment.

'It will be a mess, won't it, sir? Most of the money tied up in the company came to Richard from Paul. If there's an older legitimate heir, where does that leave Sarah? Will Richard's will still be valid? And even if it is, what happens when Paul eventually dies?'

'God knows! As you say – it's a mess. That's why the solicitor was so unhappy about it. The lawyers always hate complicated arrangements within families, and the ones that involve trying to trace missing heirs are worst of all. But dealing with the money is their problem – ours is deciding what happens to motives.'

'Well, for a start, this missing child, whoever it turned out to be, would have a socking great motive for getting rid of Richard in the hope of eventually inheriting Paul's fortune. We'll need to do a spot of tracing ourselves.'

'Already set in motion, Ted. I've sent a request to the English police to trace all Paul's addresses and check records in those areas for the registration of a birth to an Annette Taylor.'

'There is another possibility we could try as well, sir.'

'What's that, Ted?'

'We could check the records here.'

'Why here? I thought you said Paul had never been to the islands before.'

'That's what Sarah's statement says, sir, yes. But I've got a hunch it's just possible that Paul could have been here before, all the same. It would make sense of something we'd both written off as moonshine.'

'What?'

'Your interview with Muriel Wilson. Perhaps the old lady's not so far off-beam as we thought. She's just slipped a time zone and got her generations mixed up, that's all. She said she'd seen Richard on the island in 1948, and we thought she was just rambling. But what if she really did see *Paul* when she was here on honeymoon? There was a fairly strong family resemblance between Paul and Richard, and she may just have confused her memory of Paul as a young man with the Richard she met this year.'

The Inspector nodded slowly, following the thought through.

'It would make sense. We can look for records of a marriage locally, as well as the birth of a child.'

Harris leaned forward in his chair.

'I've just had another thought! It's a long shot, and a bit too much of a coincidence perhaps – but well worth checking, all the same. Martel's wife, Claire – we don't happen to know her maiden name, do we? It couldn't possibly be Taylor, could it?'

The Inspector was less than impressed.

'Come off it, Ted! That's not just a long shot; it's a really wild guess, even by your standards. I can't remember their surname, but I'm fairly sure both Claire's parents are dead; they rebuilt the island practically from scratch after the war, and her father wasn't in the best of health to begin with – I think he died soon after Claire married Martel. There's no way he can conveniently turn out to be the same person as Paul, if that's what you were thinking.'

Harris looked disappointed for a moment, then had another thought.

'All right then – but there's no reason why Claire's *mother* couldn't have been this Annette. She might have married again, after having the child.'

He caught the Inspector's eye, and gave a wry grin.

'I know – I know! It's a bit far-fetched.'

'A bit!'

'Well – yes, all right – a lot! But it won't do any harm to check, anyway. And you have to admit, it would give us a very convincing suspect, right on the spot and with a strong motive.'

Le Sauvage sighed.

'It's never that simple! You're right, though; it's worth a try. And I agree with your instinct about the possibility of a local connection; we can go ahead and check records for any births within a likely time-span with mother's name Annette – regardless of surname. If Paul needed to specify a search for the child, that almost certainly means he'd lost touch with the mother, so calling her Annette Taylor may have been an assumption on his part. I'll set that up today. But meanwhile, there's a much more immediate approach – and much simpler.'

Harris nodded.

'Ask Paul.'

* * *

On the way back to his own office, Harris met Constable Brouard in the corridor.

'I was just coming to find you, sir. The desk sergeant wants to know if you need me on Longuey today, or whether he can use me here.'

'Not sure yet, Jim. Come with me now and I'll think about it.'

In the office, Brouard perched on the edge of the desk while Harris jotted down lists of interviews completed and still outstanding, and men available. While he waited, the constable flicked through the pile of newspapers that had accumulated as usual on Harris's desk. The Sergeant always claimed it was a vital part of police intelligence work to keep up with events in the local and national press. He believed what he said, but rarely managed to find time to practice what he preached; Brouard was often the only one who read any of the assortment of newspapers delivered each day. He was also the only one who ever got around to throwing any of them out – whenever he was away on leave the pile gradually and inexorably engulfed the whole desk like the unstoppable lava flow from a volcano.

Eventually Harris looked up.

'You can join the Longuey contingent today, I think. I wouldn't mind another word with that French chef of theirs to start with, and then you can sit in with me on an interview with Martel. The Inspector is going to tackle Blythe again, thank God. Slippery bugger, that one – I wouldn't trust myself not to lose my temper with him.'

Brouard grinned.

'M.P.s are meant to be slippery these days, sir. That's what makes them successful. They probably wouldn't last five minutes at Westminster if they told the truth all the time.'

'Blythe will last a damn sight longer than five minutes, then, if I'm any judge,' grunted Harris. 'In fact, he'll probably go far,' he added sourly.

'All the way to the top,' agreed Brouard, easing himself off the edge of the desk. 'He's strongly fancied for a cabinet post soon, they say. He's certainly made his mark at the Department of the Environment – in spite of having to slide out from under the effects of that pesticide scandal last year. He's a survivor, all right – I wish the Inspector joy of him today!' He made his way to the door, stopping with his fingers on the handle to ask, 'Are we going over on the ferry, or the island workboat?'

'Hmm? Oh, workboat,' said Harris absently.

'Right you are, sir. See you later, then,' said Brouard cheerfully, and went out.

It was only after the door had closed behind him that the

tumblers in Harris's mind finally clicked into the right combination to reveal the elusive thought he'd been chasing since the day before. With a turn of speed surprising in a man of his bulk, he bounded from his chair and across to the door, yanked it open, and bellowed down the corridor after the constable's retreating figure.

Back in the office again, Brouard found Harris scattering papers from the case file all over the desk, and muttering, 'Pesticides, you cloth-head, that was it – pesticides!'

'Beg pardon, sir?'

'Neville Blythe,' said Harris, still rummaging in the file, 'you just said something about Neville Blythe and a pesticides scandal last year. Can you fill me in on the details?'

'Oh, I see. Got you, sir.'

Brouard himself began rummaging on the desk, and Harris looked up briefly from his own paper-chase in astonishment.

'What in heaven's name are you up to, lad?' he barked. 'I asked you a simple question – it wasn't an invitation to join a treasure-hunt!'

'Sorry, sir. Newspapers, sir,' explained Brouard.

'Eh?'

'Newspapers. It was one of the newspapers I was looking through just now that reminded me about it. There was a follow-up article; if I can just find which paper it was in, I'll read it to you. Ah, yes – here we are. I'm sure it was in this one.'

He picked out one of the papers and folded it to an inside page.

Meanwhile, Harris appeared to have completed his own search; as he sat and listened, he cleared a space on the desk in front of him and opened out the particular sheet he'd tracked down from the papers in the file, trying unsuccessfully to brush off a large muddy paw-print in one corner.

Brouard cleared his throat and began reading:

'A new scientific report published today re-opens many of the questions raised last year on the safety of some recently developed organochlorine pesticides and chlorinated biphenyls ...'

Harris groaned.

'All right, you can stop there for the moment. I remember now why I didn't pay enough attention to all the fuss about this lot last time around. It was the Pooh Bear effect.'

'Sir?'

'I am a bear of very little brain,' explained Harris wearily, 'and long words bother me. I tell you what – you're supposed to be the one with the education; why don't you just give me a précis?'

'What's a précis, sir?' asked Brouard innocently.

'Bloody G.C.S.E's!' exploded Harris, and then caught the broad grin on Brouard's face and subsided into a mutter. 'All right, all right – so you're winding me up. I still say I'd like to see you tackle an old O-Level English paper, but let that pass – for the moment. Just give me the gist of the bit about the pesticides.'

'Well, there's a whole group of new ones been developed over the last year or so. What everyone's looking for is something that will be effective without being destructive to the environment or causing long-term health scares.'

Harris nodded.

'I know – big problem. I've got one of those environmentally-friendly insecticides at home, for spraying my roses. Approved by Greenpeace, Friends of the Earth and probably the Women's Institute as well, I shouldn't wonder.

Guaranteed non-toxic to man, beast, bird and butterfly. Wonderful stuff – only one snag.'

'What's that, sir?'

'It's also non-toxic to greenfly!' said Harris gloomily. 'My roses are still smothered in them. Never known a summer like it.'

'Exactly!' said Brouard. 'And that's why the farmers are getting worried.'

'Never knew a farmer when he wasn't,' interrupted Harris. 'Never satisfied whatever happens, farmers. Proper moaning minnies, the lot of them.'

'It's global warming,' persisted Brouard, ignoring the Sergeant's mutterings. 'Conditions get more and more favourable to pests, and they multiply out of control. At the same time, there's more and more evidence of the harm some chemicals do to the environment, so you can't use things like D.D.T. any more. Latest scare is that a lot of these chemicals may be responsible for lowering sperm counts, as well as possibly causing some cancers; that's what this article's mainly about.'

'Bloody hell!' said Harris. 'Perhaps the farmers have got something to moan about, after all. Where does our friend Blythe fit in to all this, then?'

'Well, for a start, there's seriously big money waiting to be made here – the first chemical company to come up with a really effective pesticide that's also completely safe will be on to a gold-mine, with huge sales potential worldwide. And last year it looked as if there might have been a breakthrough – a product was announced that was lethal to several major agricultural pests, and seemed to be non-toxic to humans. Blythe appeared to give it the official approval of the Department of the Environment – made a speech at one point about how wonderful it was that a British company was in the forefront of what he called 'the new agricultural revolution'. Only he jumped the gun, rather. It turned out the product hadn't been thoroughly tested before release, and it showed up some rather horrific side-effects in use – caused blisters and skin damage in farmers handling it regularly. The chemical had to be withdrawn, and there are compensation cases still going on. Blythe only wriggled out from his connection with it because of his natural caution – apparently when you look at the detail of what he said in the speech, there's nowhere you can actually pin him down to a definite endorsement of the product itself. The heavyweight press tried to imply he had some financial link with the company that made it, but they could never prove anything, and Blythe stuck to his guns and ignored any suggestions that he ought to resign; the P.M. backed him and it all blew over when a bigger scandal broke the following week. It must have been a scare for Blythe, though – I bet he wished he'd never heard of the wretched chemical – can't remember what it was called, now, but it probably says in here …'

He ran his finger down the article in the newspaper, but Harris beat him to it.

'Phenthane,' he said quietly.

Brouard looked up, startled.

'Yes, that was it! How did you know that?'

'I knew it rang a bell from somewhere when I read it last night, only I couldn't place it. It's on here, Jim,' He tapped his finger lightly on the paper in front of him, 'On the list of products developed by one of Richard Taylor's companies!'

Brouard whistled.

'That's interesting. So there probably was a previous connection between Blythe and Taylor – and one that they'd both want hushed up, especially Blythe. What if Richard tried a spot of blackmail? That would give Blythe a powerful motive to get rid of him'

'True. But lets not run before we can walk. We're a long way from proving anything.'

'It certainly gives us something new to think about, though.'

'Doesn't it just!' said Harris.

* * *

It was half an hour later, when Harris was back at his own desk gulping a hurried cup of coffee before going to join the team heading for the boat to Longuey, that the news came in of the discovery of Abigail's body.

# CHAPTER 17

The events of the rest of the morning flowed past Robbie in a dream-like sequence, like the scenes of a play he had somehow found himself performing in without ever having seen the full script. Parts of it were dreadfully familiar: the grim expression on Bernard's face when he heard the news; the sending out of the men in a small boat; the struggle to recover the body, with the boat perilously close to the rocks; the wait for the arrival of the police. It was like a nightmare that recurs with slight variations in detail but the same underlying horror. Robbie knew that he should stay in the hotel to be available to the police when they arrived, but he felt that he couldn't bear to be interviewed again, probably by the same Sergeant; he had to break the pattern.

He slipped out of the hotel and headed through the mist that still swirled fitfully across the paths and curled round the shrubs and trees in the garden. As he went, he tried to convince himself that his absence wouldn't be noticed. After all, it wasn't as if he was the sole witness this time – there was a whole boat-load of people who had all seen the body at the same time, so there was nothing he could add to anything they would tell the police. Somewhere at the back of his mind lurked the thought that if he could only avoid talking to the police about this second death, it would turn out not to have happened at all. He couldn't cope with the memory of Abigail as she had been last night, and equate it with the thing in the water this morning.

He didn't want to think about it. He didn't want to think at all. All he wanted to do was hide. He couldn't stop the thoughts coming, though, even as he tramped doggedly along the paths heading for his secret place. They weren't thoughts of Abigail's death at all, but of Richard's. He could push the new horror to the back of his mind, but only at the expense of bringing the old one back into focus, with all its attendant dark reflections. However hard he tried to stop them, the thoughts strung themselves together into sequences: his father's expensive plans for the island's development; Richard's money, and the long secret sessions in the office; the expression on his mother's face as she said the plans wouldn't be able to go ahead – 'not now'; the empty bed at the cottage in the early morning silence.

It all made a horrible twisted sense, and the pieces began to fit together into a picture he didn't want to look at. To distract his mind from the conclusions he was so afraid to draw, he quickened his pace and began to count his footsteps, concentrating on muttering the numbers to himself like some protective mantra.

'Fifty-seven, fifty-eight, fifty-nine … ouch!'

His foot hit a rabbit hole and twisted underneath him, and he went sprawling sideways into a tangle of brambles and nettles. He rubbed angrily at his elbow, which had hit the ground first and hardest as he went down, and felt the prickle of tears gathering behind his eyelids to match the prickle of the nettle-stings on his hands and ankles.

'Are you all right?'

He looked up in embarrassment, and hastily rubbed a hand across his eyes so that the tears remained unshed.

The figure reaching down a hand to help him up looked very familiar, but for the moment he couldn't quite place the face.

'What bad luck, falling into all those nettles. Why don't you test the ankle to check it's not sprained or anything, and I'll look for some dock leaves – there are usually some about, somewhere near nettle clumps.'

It was the voice that brought recognition, though he'd last heard it speaking French. His mouth gaped open in surprise as he watched her searching the undergrowth beside the path for dock leaves. It was the French publisher's girl-friend – but looking completely different; it wasn't surprising he hadn't recognised her immediately. She wore dark jeans and a faded blue sweater, and her hair swung loose around her face instead of being scraped severely back. Without make-up her face was softer and more relaxed. She managed to look at the same time both older and younger than that artificial Barbie-doll figure he had watched in the hotel lounge the night before. She also looked very much happier.

She handed him a bunch of dock leaves. He rubbed them on the nettle stings and almost immediately felt the prickling begin to fade. She smiled at him.

'It's amazing how well it works, isn't it?'

Still rubbing, he smiled back.

'Thanks.'

She shrugged.

'I'm sure you'd have found them for yourself.'

She hesitated, on the verge of turning away. Robbie suddenly felt the need for company, and conversation, to stop the dark thoughts from returning. He wasn't so sure now that his original instinct, to run and hide, was a such a good one after all. Alone in the tunnel, wouldn't he just be overwhelmed by all his fears and suspicions?

He threw away the bruised and crumpled dock leaves. The backs of his hands were stained a yellowish green now, and he could still feel the stings, but only faintly.

'I didn't expect to meet anyone on this path,' he said. 'Most people don't realise it's here at all.'

'I was surprised to meet anyone, too. I found this route last week, when I was out for an early-morning walk round the island.'

'Do you often go for early walks?'

'Oh yes! It's really beautiful in the very early morning. I can't understand why so many people sleep so late. They often miss the very best of the day.'

She smiled, and Robbie thought that she wasn't at all bad-looking, actually. He remembered seeing the publisher waiting for the ferry to Guernsey earlier in the morning, and guessed that she'd taken the opportunity, in his absence, to escape from the facade she felt obliged to maintain for his benefit. Robbie wondered why she bothered, when it so clearly didn't make her happy. But then, adults did some pretty stupid things sometimes.

They walked on together in companionable silence. It seemed to have been taken for granted now that their paths, having met, shouldn't separate again. When they reached the point in the path where the route to the tunnel branched off, Robbie walked on past it without a sideways glance.

'You go walking early as well, don't you?' she said, 'I saw you, I think, earlier in the week.'

'I go swimming early, too,' said Robbie. 'The sea's often beautifully calm first thing in the morning. Or in the evening, sometimes, whatever the weather's been like during the day.

But I think the morning's best. The earlier the better, really – as soon as it's light. Or even before, so that you can watch the sun come up.'

She laughed.

'It must run in the family.'

Robbie looked puzzled.

'What?'

'Your mother's sometimes up very early, too, isn't she? Well, she certainly was the morning I met her at the pottery.'

Robbie became aware of his heart beating, and it seemed to him to be going very fast.

'Which morning was that?' he asked, trying to keep the tremble out of his voice. She thought for a moment.

'It was the same day that poor man was found drowned. I remember noticing how tired your mother looked at dinner that night, and thinking what a long and difficult day she must have had, starting off so early in the morning and then having a death to cope with.'

She fell silent, and Robbie wondered how to phrase a question to make her go on, but it wasn't necessary; after a while she continued without prompting.

'It wasn't a very promising morning for a walk, that day – it was obviously going to rain later. But I couldn't sleep, and I thought I might as well see if I could beat the clouds and get some fresh air, anyway. I met your mother on her way to the pottery, and she said she couldn't sleep either and had decided to get some work done. I went with her, and she showed me round the pottery and made me a cup of coffee, and then we chatted while she worked. She told me a lot about you, actually. She's very proud of you, you know.'

'I know,' said Robbie, conscious of straightforward embarrassment overlaying the enormous sense of relief that was suddenly, wonderfully, flooding through him. It was all right; his stupid suspicions were all rot; everything was simple and exactly as his mother had said it was, and there was nothing to worry about after all. Somewhere in the very depths of his mind a still small voice was trying to point out that it wasn't quite *that* simple, but in his new state of confidence he had no difficulty at all in suppressing it.

* * *

By the time they got back to the hotel a stiff breeze had sprung up, and the mist had given way to drizzle building up into steady rain. As they reached the gate into the gardens, the rain became even heavier, and the wind more gusty. They sprinted up the path and tumbled through the front door, their hair sodden and their cheeks whipped into redness by the wind.

'I'll look out for you, next time I'm out early,' said Robbie.

She brushed back a strand of hair that was dripping water on to the end of her nose, and smiled at him.

'I'll wave,' she promised, and headed up the stairs. He wondered if she was going to change into Barbie's next outfit immediately, or if she would hang on to her own identity until the last possible moment; as she saw the ferry pulling in to the harbour below, perhaps. Once again, he marvelled at the strangeness of adults.

The lounge door opened and Bernard and Claire came out.

Robbie found himself thinking that it was the first time he'd actually seen the two of them together since the evening of Richard's death. Perhaps what was needed to get his parents speaking to one another on a more regular basis was a whole string of deaths – a serial killer at loose on the island might do it. Even as he formulated the thought, he was surprised and disgusted with himself; he was getting worse even than Hal at his most cynical. He stood and dripped on to the hall carpet, and felt some of his new-found confidence sliding off him with the rainwater.

'I'm glad you're here, Robbie,' said Claire. 'We thought you might have gone back to the cottage. Why don't you go and dry yourself off a bit in the downstairs cloakroom and then come back and find us. The police are here. They're busy interviewing other people at the moment, but Sergeant Harris would like a word with you later, if you can bear it.'

'Oh yes,' thought Robbie, 'I can bear it. It's amazing what you can bear when you really have to.'

# CHAPTER 18

Jean-Pierre was clearly not happy at the prospect of being interviewed again, and Brouard immediately began eyeing him with ill-concealed suspicion, but the Sergeant was more open minded; he realised the chef was probably just frustrated to be away from the kitchen so near to lunch-time. Cooks were very like policemen, really, he thought – most of them found it difficult to delegate.

Jean-Pierre's first words confirmed Harris's instincts.

'Will this take very long? There are things in the kitchen that I must supervise, you understand.'

'I'll be as brief as I can. But we must be thorough – this is a death we're investigating. Two deaths, in fact.'

Jean-Pierre raised an eyebrow.

'You think there may be some connection – between the deaths of Mlle. Meredith and M. Taylor?'

'We don't know at this stage. But it may be a possibility. So you must forgive me if I begin by going over your previous statement, briefly.'

The chef glanced at his watch and frowned, but made no further protest. Harris took him through his account of the recovery of Richard's body.

'That is correct, Sergeant. It is all as I have told you before.'

'Is there anything you may be able to add, now that you've had time to think about it? Or in the light of this new death, perhaps? Anything that you might have noticed, even if it didn't strike you as relevant at the time.'

Jean-Pierre frowned.

'Perhaps ... but no – it is nothing.'

'Let me be the judge of that, please. Tell us anything at all that occurs to you, even if it seems trivial.'

'Not trivial, no – but unconnected, surely. They were just meetings, that is all.'

'What meetings?'

There was a distinct pause before Jean-Pierre continued, speaking slowly as if choosing his words carefully.

'There are always many meetings here – business meetings. People come over from the mainland for business lunches and conferences; they are very popular, naturally – my food is very good. And for smaller, more personal meetings, there is usually coffee, and my special pastries.'

'So you're always likely to know about meetings that are going on,' prompted Harris gently, when Jean-Pierre fell silent.

'Of course. M. Bernard knows that he can trust my discretion. Some meetings are very private.'

Again, silence. Harris wondered whether to intervene, but eventually the chef seemed to make up his mind.

'It was the English politician, M. Blythe,' he said. 'He was in a long meeting with M. Taylor – the young M. Taylor, M. Richard – the day before the death. It was just after lunch. They had had coffee, and I went to ask if they wanted more.

M. Blythe was angry that I interrupted them. He was very rude.'

'Was that unusual?' asked Harris, thinking that insolence to the lower orders had probably been bred into Neville Blythe.

'It was unnecessary,' said Jean-Pierre, with some dignity. 'I did not enter without knocking, and I overheard nothing. Yes, M. Blythe is often rude; he is not a true gentleman, I think – but in my experience that is often the case with the English.'

Harris dared not look at Brouard; he felt the constable bristling, and prayed that he could control himself. Jean-Pierre continued unperturbed,

'But there is a difference between natural arrogance and the rudeness that comes from anger. I asked myself what could be the subject of this meeting that would make M. Blythe lose his temper so quickly at being interrupted.'

'But you say you overheard nothing.'

'Nothing at all.'

'What was Richard Taylor's reaction. Was he angry too?'

'Not angry, no.'

'What, then?'

'I think he was afraid.'

'Do you mean he was frightened by your interruption, or do you think he was already afraid when you entered the room?'

Jean-Pierre shrugged.

'I cannot say. Perhaps fear is too strong a word; it may have been only nervousness. It was only an impression. I do not want to make it important when it may be nothing. As I said before – it was just a meeting.'

'Meetings,' said Harris softly.

'Pardon?'

'What you said before, if I remember rightly, was, 'They were just meetings.' Isn't that right, Constable?'

Brouard turned back a page in his notes, and nodded.

'That's right, sir. Definitely meetings, in the plural.'

Harris leaned forward.

'So would you like to tell us what other meetings Richard Taylor was involved in, in the days before his death?'

Jean-Pierre frowned.

'There were others, yes, but they were not remarkable – not like the one I have just told you.'

'We need to hear about them, all the same. Anything he did in the time he was here at the hotel before his death may turn out to be significant.'

There was a long pause, and Harris felt his patience beginning to slip.

'I have to remind you, Jean-Pierre, that you have a duty to help us to the best of your ability. Holding things back from the police in a murder investigation is a very serious matter.'

This time Jean-Pierre was startled into an immediate response.

'Murder? Are you really certain about that, Sergeant? Surely it was an accident, the death of M. Taylor?'

'There are indications of suspicious circumstances. So let's have a little more cooperation, please. Just tell us about the meetings.'

'There were several,' admitted Jean-Pierre reluctantly. 'With M. Bernard, and with M. Blythe.'

'Separately, or together?'

'Both. Separate meetings first, then all three of them together.'

'Did you know what these meetings were about?'

Once again, Jean-Pierre hesitated.

'It can have no connection with your investigations, I think.'

'With respect, that's not for you to decide. We need all the facts before we can decide which ones are relevant.'

'I cannot give you definite facts, Sergeant; only my own opinion, from what I had observed and the little I had been told directly – in confidence, you understand. That is why I was perhaps reluctant to tell you.'

'Nevertheless ...' prompted Harris, and Jean-Pierre sighed.

'Nevertheless, Sergeant, I see now that indeed I must speak. It was a plan for the development of Longuey – very extensive development. A plan that would require much money, I think. Money from the politician, and perhaps from M. Taylor's company; I do not know. But M. Bernard told me something of his intentions, because he needed to know if I would stay on as chef.'

He gave a brief outline of the scheme for the marina complex and the casino. Harris's eyes widened in surprise at the scale of the proposals.

'And what did you tell him – about staying on?'

'I told him that I did not know. There would have been big changes. He gave me time to make up my mind. But now – who knows what will happen now?'

'What about Mrs. Martel?' asked Harris, remembering the signs of strain he had noticed in the relationship between Bernard and Claire, 'Was she included in these plans? Did she approve of them?'

'She was not involved in any of the meetings.' said Jean-Pierre.

Harris noted that he had only answered part of the question, but decided not to pursue it. There was more here to be probed later, but this was a distraction from the more immediate matter in hand.

'All right, Jean-Pierre, let's move on to the second death – Miss Abigail Meredith's.'

He couldn't be sure, but he thought he detected a slight relaxation of tension, as if this were more comfortable ground.

'But of course. A terrible misfortune, to fall in the fog like that; it is a tragedy – she was such a beautiful girl. I think I may be able to help you, Sergeant. Since her body was found this morning, I have thought much about it. and I think I must have been one of the last people to see her last night, setting out on her way up the path to her death, poor girl.'

'You saw her? Outside the hotel? At what time?'

'At about half past ten, I think, or perhaps a little later. The light was fading, and also it was difficult to see because of the fog. But I am sure that the person I saw was Mlle. Meredith. She came out of the front door of the hotel and went through the garden to the start of the private cliff path.'

'And where were you?'

'In the little summer-house at the edge of the lawn beside the swimming pool. She passed quite close, but she didn't see us.'

'Us? There was someone with you?'

Jean-Pierre smiled.

'I had an assignation,' he said, 'But it is not allowed – a liaison between a member of staff and a hotel guest. So we have to be discreet; that is why we met in the summer-house.'

'Did you see anyone else?'

He hesitated, remembering.

'There *was* someone, a little later. Perhaps ten minutes later, I think; we heard someone else moving through the garden. But even in ten minutes, the light had faded and the fog was thicker; it was difficult to see clearly. It was a shadow – no more.'

'Man, or woman?'

'Impossible to say. Wearing trousers, yes, I'm sure – but of course it could still have been either.'

'Coming from the hotel?'

'Not through the front door. Round the side of the building.'

'So it could have been someone coming out of the back door of the hotel, or from outside the grounds through the back gate?'

'Yes. Or through the side door from the kitchen block.'

'You saw no-one else? Later, perhaps?'

'No. We did not stay in the summer-house much longer. It was dark, and getting very cold.'

'You realise that I'll need to talk to your companion?'

'Is that really necessary? We have been so careful to avoid trouble until now.'

'I'm sure you can rely on our discretion. If you just give me the young lady's name, we only need to check that she confirms your statement.'

'I'm sorry, Sergeant, but it is not possible for me to do that.'

Harris was on the verge of losing his temper when he caught the tone of amusement in the voice. He looked at the sardonic expression on Jean-Pierre's classically handsome features, and a grin of understanding slowly spread across his own face.

'All right,' he said, 'My mistake. Just tell me who he is, and if his account agrees with yours, I'll see what I can do about keeping it under wraps.'

* * *

'Wow!' said Brouard, when Jean-Pierre had been released back to the kitchen. 'We got rather more than we bargained for there!'

Harris nodded, still grinning.

'It takes all sorts,' he said. 'Do me a favour – next time I jump to conclusions about a Frenchman, lean over and whisper "Jean-Pierre" in my ear. Not the best of witnesses, what with the fog and the obvious distractions, but still useful information. And the earlier stuff was interesting, too.'

'Like getting blood out of a stone, though, the bit about the plans for the island. Why should he be so reluctant for us to find out about that, I wonder?'

'Loyalty to the family.' said Harris briefly, his mind working overtime.

'Come on, sir,' protested Brouard, 'That won't wash. If he wanted to do Bernard a favour, he should have been falling over himself to tell us about it, once we'd mentioned murder. I mean, if Richard was going to be putting up a fair chunk of the money, where's Bernard's motive for getting rid of him? He's hardly likely to kill the goose that's providing half the golden eggs, is he?'

'You're not thinking it through far enough, Jim,' said Harris sadly. 'I didn't say loyalty to Bernard, I said loyalty to the family – to what Jean-Pierre sees as the family tradition. Remember he's stayed on here as chef for a long time, when he could probably have got a more high-powered job on the mainland by now, with his experience. He's stayed because he likes the set-up here; likes it as it is at the moment. I can't see him going along with Bernard's ambitions to turn this place into a copy of Las Vegas. No, it's not Bernard he's trying to protect. It's someone who I suspect is passionately opposed to everything Bernard wants to do.'

Brouard sounded surprised, then doubtful.

'Claire, you mean? Claire trying to preserve the character of the island? It's a motive, I suppose, but is it strong enough? Could she actually kill someone, just to stop a business deal going through, however much she disapproved of it?'

'I don't know,' admitted Harris. 'It seems unlikely, I grant you. But I've been in this game long enough to know that the unlikely often turns out to be true. You look at Claire Martel and you see a likeable character, an efficient business-woman and a loving mother; you don't *want* her to be a killer, so you say she's not capable of it. But *anyone* is capable of killing if something they care about deeply enough is threatened. And you have to admit, it does seem unlikely after Richard's death that the development scheme will survive – I can't see Blythe sticking with it now, especially with this second death too close for comfort. He'll be too busy covering his own back. So everything has turned out just as Claire would have hoped.'

'You mean, Bernard won't be able to go ahead with his plans?'

'No, he won't,' said Harris, unconsciously echoing Claire's words to Robbie, 'Not now.'

# CHAPTER 19

He was disguising it well, but there was no doubt about it; this time Neville Blythe was seriously rattled. Le Sauvage noted the tiny twitching muscle underneath one aristocratic cheek-bone, and the faintest beading of sweat on the classically chiselled upper lip. Blythe's voice was still under complete control, but the Inspector didn't miss the slight tremble of the paper as the M.P. turned over the last page of his statement.

'What happens now, Inspector? Do I sign it? And then may I go?'

'All in good time, sir. We want to make quite sure that we're both satisfied nothing has been left out.'

'I don't think it's very likely that anything's been missed.' said Blythe drily.'You've been very thorough, Inspector. I congratulate you.'

'I think it's a little early for congratulations, sir. I was very thorough in my questions last time, if you remember; it was the answers that turned out to be rather less than complete on that occasion.'

Blythe flushed an angry red.

'There's no need to bring that up again. I've admitted I was evasive about the boat. That was very wrong of me, and I've already apologised. But you have to understand my position. I had to do all I could to avoid involvement in any scandal.'

'Oh, I think I understand your position well enough, sir. In fact, I think I understand it rather better than you appear to do yourself. I can assure you, you have rather more to worry about at the moment than just a possible involvement in scandal.'

'Surely not. An unfortunate coincidence of circumstances, I grant you; two tragic accidents on one small island within a week. But simple accidents, nevertheless. Sadly, these things just happen.'

The Inspector looked Blythe squarely in the eye and said quietly,

'You think so?'

He hoped the absence of the word "sir" had been noted.

Blythe looked steadily back and said, equally quietly,

'Of course, Inspector. Don't you?'

Le Sauvage let the silence between them lengthen to the point where a weaker man might have begun to crack, but Blythe remained impassive; only the treacherous cheek muscle still betrayed him.

'All right,' said the Inspector at last, 'let's take the young lady's death first, since your account of that is quite straightforward. You say she just went out of your room at some time after dinner and you never saw her again. Didn't you worry when she didn't come back?'

'I never worried about Abigail. She wasn't that sort of girl. She was quite capable of taking care of herself, and she always did exactly what she felt like doing. There was simply no point in worrying about her – it wouldn't make a scrap of difference.'

'I'm not so sure of that. She clearly couldn't take care of herself last night. She ended up dead.'

'As I said – a tragic accident. She decided to go for a walk and lost her balance on the cliff-edge in the fog. A little surprising, perhaps – she was usually very sure-footed. But nothing sinister, Inspector. If it wasn't for the fact that it was the second death in a week, you probably wouldn't be taking such a detailed interest in it.'

The Inspector, remembering the Chief-Superintendent and the Commissioner, thought that this was probably true.

'You're sure she didn't say anything about where she was going, or whether she was expecting to meet anyone?'

'Quite sure.'

'And you didn't go out yourself at any time after dinner last night?'

'I've told you already. You've got it written down. No, I didn't. I don't know why you need me to say it again. You said it yourself – it's all quite straightforward.'

'All right, then. Let's go back to the bit that's not so straightforward. Tell me again about the boat.'

* * *

'I should warn you, we already know about the boat,' said Harris, and Bernard let out a sigh that could almost have been relief.

'I wanted to tell you,' he said, 'I really did. But it was difficult.'

He stopped, and Harris waited patiently for him to continue. The Sergeant had enough experience to recognise the moment when a further question was unnecessary. Martel had made up his mind this time to tell the truth – though perhaps still not the whole truth. Prompting at this stage was not appropriate; might even be counter-productive. He was quite prepared for this interview to take a long time.

Eventually, Bernard spoke again.

'It was stupid of me,' he said. 'I knew really that you'd probably be able to trace the movements of the boat. But it's a busy time of year, and I know the records aren't always accurate to the exact day, with comings and goings after dark, so it was worth a try. I suppose someone saw us arrive at St Peterport – or my boat coming back?'

The Sergeant didn't answer, and Bernard shrugged.

'Well, it doesn't matter, anyway, does it, now? The important thing is that I lied, and you know that I lied. I felt bad about the lying at the time, but I didn't know then that Richard's death was anything but an accident. Ever since Claire told me about the inquest, I've been trying to find the courage to come to you. I'm sorry I didn't manage it before you came to me first. But I swear to you now, if I'd had any idea at the time that there was any possibility of it being murder, I would never have agreed to try to cover anything up.'

Harris nodded. It was good to have his instincts confirmed; he'd always felt the suggestion to conceal the truth hadn't come from Martel himself. He let the silence continue while Bernard gathered his thoughts to begin again.

'There were five of us on the boat that night. It was something of a celebration, really. We'd put together a consortium for a very promising scheme for the development of parts of the island – Richard, Neville Blythe and myself. It had all been finalised that evening in the hotel, and we'd been discussing it until late into the night. Abigail's always a night-bird, and Sarah had been up very late with Richard's father.

They both came downstairs looking for us, and found us all about to crack open the champagne. I can't remember now whose idea it was to transfer to the boat. Probably Abigail's. Sarah seemed doubtful, but in the end she agreed, and we took the champagne with us and took the boat out, and anchored in the most secluded bay, well away from the harbour. Then we opened the first bottle.'

He stopped again, and rested his head on one hand, massaging the skin above his eyebrows with his thumb and forefinger as if trying to ease a headache, his whole body taut with the strain of remembering.

'I don't know how long we stayed there, drinking and talking. Abigail was pretty wild – she may well have been high on something before she joined us, and she was knocking the champagne back hard and fast. Sarah was tired and subdued, and didn't drink much, but I have to admit the rest of us were fairly far gone by the time Richard went out on deck.'

Bernard fell silent again, and Harris decided that this time a question was necessary.

'Did anyone go out with him?'

'I've tried to think, but I honestly don't know. I've said – I was quite knocked out myself by then. I don't drink much, usually – it's not a good idea, when you're in the hotel business – and champagne goes straight to my head. I don't even have a very clear recollection of him actually going out; it was more just a realisation that he wasn't in the cabin with the rest of us any more. I don't think anyone else followed him out, but I couldn't swear to it. You'll have to ask the others.'

Harris thought grimly that he couldn't ask Abigail, but all he said was, 'We will, sir. Go on.'

'I am trying to remember, but it gets confused. I vaguely

remember hearing splashing, and cries for help, but the next thing I have a clear memory of is being out on deck, and all of us struggling to get Richard out of the water, and then fighting to try to revive him. It was a nightmare.'

'Who gave him artificial respiration?'

'I did. I'm trained in first aid – it's one of my many responsibilities on the island. I gave him mouth-to-mouth, and Abigail kept the heart massage going. She knew exactly what to do and did it very capably, in spite of having given the impression previously of being stoned out of her mind – she's a dark horse, that girl.'

He stopped abruptly, remembering.

'Oh God – she's dead too, now!'

'We'll come to that later,' said Harris, not unkindly, 'Try not to worry about it for the moment. Go on telling me what happened on the boat.'

'I don't know how long we went on trying to revive him – it felt like hours, but of course it can't have been. It was Abigail who eventually said there was no point in going on any longer. I remember I didn't want to stop, although I knew she was right – I just didn't want to have to admit he was dead. When we did stop, I remember the silence – we were all stunned, and nobody said a word for a long time; all you could hear was the lapping of the water against the side of the boat.'

'Who started the panic?' asked the Sergeant quietly.

'Sarah,' said Bernard immediately, and Harris nodded, his instinct proved right.

'She went to pieces. All of a sudden, she was sobbing and wailing, and Abigail was trying to calm her down, and Neville lost his temper and was shouting at both of them to shut up and let him think. It was pandemonium. I was trying to make them all hush, because I wasn't sure how far the sound would carry, over water and at night. It was awful – there was Richard, lying dead on the deck, and all I could think of was that nobody else must hear the row they were making.'

He stopped, and again Harris gave him time; time to go on remembering, and to think. When he continued, his voice was lower, and the words came slowly and with a measure of pain.

'I suppose I was already thinking about the bad publicity – how the thing would look. It was Neville who insisted we had to find some way to keep him completely out of it, but I didn't do anything to try to dissuade him; I'm really as much to blame as he is for the things we eventually did, and the trouble it caused you.'

'What about the others? Did you all discuss it together?'

'It wasn't exactly what you'd call a rational discussion. We were all too confused and upset and frightened to make much sense. But we did all agree, yes. Even Sarah. I've wondered about that since, as a matter of fact – but it didn't seem at all strange to me at the time. I suppose she was just swept along by Neville. He's a very forceful personality, you know. He and Abigail dreamed up the whole thing between them. She was excited; almost enjoying herself – like a little girl absorbed in a game. She was the one who suggested the footprints. Neville insisted we had to make it look like a swimming accident, so that it wasn't so obvious Richard had gone into the water from a boat, but then it was Abigail who worked out that with the tide going out, we could fake footprints from the beach.'

'Whose footprints were they?'

'Mine. We'd taken the clothes off Richard's body – not an experience I'd ever wish to repeat, I can tell you; stripping wet clothes from a corpse – but then we realised we'd need his swimming trunks, as well as a set of his clothes from his room. I had the keys to the back door of the hotel, and we thought it would be safer to let the women in that way – it was well past one o'clock by this time, but it was just possible there might still be someone about. So Neville stayed with the boat and I took Abigail and Sarah back in the dinghy. We took Richard's wet clothes with us. We got back to the hotel without meeting anyone, and Sarah gave me the swimming trunks and the new set of clothes – she even remembered to grab a towel from the bathroom.'

'She didn't quite think of everything, though, did she?'

'No. I should have thought of shoes, but I didn't – probably because we hadn't brought his wet ones back with us. I don't know what happened to them, come to think of it – I suppose Neville must have just flung them over the side. Even so, I should have thought of shoes … but I didn't. Even when I took off my own shoes later, on the beach, I didn't see the significance. But I wasn't thinking straight at all by then – the whole thing was like something out of a dream. It was only the next morning that I began to see how crazy the whole idea had been.'

'How exactly did you manage the footprints?'

'I took the dinghy back to the boat and picked Neville up, and he dropped me off at the next beach along the coast, which has a strip of shingle that doesn't show footprints. He took the dinghy back to meet me again, and I went up over the cliff path and down the steps to the beach.'

'How could you see what you were doing?'

'With difficulty – but there was just enough moonlight to find my way, and Neville had a torch and was shining it towards the beach from the dinghy. I left the clothes and the towel on a rock, took off my own shoes and carried them, and rolled my trousers up. Then all I had to do was walk out over the clear expanse of wet sand and wade out to the dinghy.'

'Leaving the clothes and footprints neatly set up to look like a night swim?'

'Yes.'

'All ready to be discovered the next morning?'

'Yes.'

'By Robbie?'

Bernard groaned and buried his head in his hands. When he looked up again, the stricken look on his face was so intense that Harris felt an involuntary pang of sympathy.

'I didn't think of that – not at the time. You've got to believe me about that, Sergeant, even if you're not convinced by anything else I say; I know it sounds unlikely, but I swear I never remembered that Robbie would be arriving for his swim the next morning. I was thinking the footprints and the clothes would be discovered much later – when the first day trippers arrived, perhaps, or someone from the hotel. The tide would have turned by then, but it wouldn't have come back in far enough to reach the footprints again. There was so much on my mind – and so much still to do, with Neville's boat to be taken across to Guernsey, towing mine to get us back. I just never thought of Robbie at all until ...'

'Until when?' prompted Harris gently.

'Until we'd got back to the hotel, in the early hours of the morning, and I'd finally gone through the motions of going to bed – though I knew there was no way I was ever going to be able to sleep. That was when I began to think about all sorts of other things; the plans for the island development, my family problems. It was only then that I remembered Robbie – that he'd already come home, and that he always goes swimming in that bay on the first day he's back. I actually got up and rushed outside in a panic when I did remember that –

but by that time it was far too late to change anything. I just had to go back into the hotel, and sit and wait for morning. I think those few hours until Robbie's phone call were the worst I've ever been through in my entire life.'

His voice cracked and his shoulders shook as he finally broke down, and Harris nodded at the constable to stop the tape-recorder and break off the interview.

* * *

Later, when the interviewing team had been provided with a late lunch of sandwiches and coffee, Harris and Le Sauvage met briefly to compare notes. The picture that emerged from the accounts given by Neville and Bernard was beginning to make a coherent whole, and they were both pleased with the progress of the case. They allowed themselves the luxury of a brief relaxation over a second cup of coffee in the lounge.

Harris reached for the sugar bowl on the table and the Inspector frowned disapprovingly.

'I thought you were supposed to have given up sugar in your coffee, Ted.'

'A vicious rumour, sir,' said Harris cheerfully, adding a second spoonful and stirring vigorously, 'spread through the station by Brouard. Fortunately, I don't let it worry me!'

'I would, if I had your blood pressure,' said Le Sauvage quietly, and Harris had the grace to look sheepish.

'All right – I know. I *am* trying to cut down, as a matter of fact, but it's not easy. I keep forgetting, in the heat of the moment. When I'm depressed, I need the comfort of something sweet to cheer me up. And when I'm in a good mood, I just think "what the hell!" – so I can't really win.'

Le Sauvage, who stayed as thin as a whippet whatever he ate, shrugged without sympathy.

'Your funeral, Ted.'

'Not quite yet, sir, I hope. Anyway, I think we've earned a spot of self-indulgence today. A good morning's work, wouldn't you say?'

'Not bad. The picture's getting a bit clearer, certainly.'

'Rather more than that, sir, surely? I fancy I could put a name to our killer – for the first murder, at any rate.'

'Finding a name is one thing – proving it is a different matter. That may not be so easy. We've made a good start, I grant you. But there's a limit to what we can do here. We'll need to transfer the interrogations back to the main incident room, where we've got all the facilities set up.'

'Tough on the Martel family – what will happen to the running of the island, with Bernard on the mainland?'

'No idea. He should have thought of that before he lied to us.'

The Inspector drained his coffee cup and got up, just as Constable Brouard came into the lounge clutching a sheet of paper.

'I think you should see this, sir – it just came in on the fax machine in the office.'

'What is it, Constable?'

'It's the results of the search of local records, sir – they've found Annette Taylor!'

Brouard passed the paper to Le Sauvage, but couldn't resist the temptation to tell them the contents before he could read it.

'The record of her marriage is there, to Paul Taylor. But there was no trace of a birth registered to an Annette Taylor, so they checked the maiden name from the marriage certificate, and then they found it. She must have reverted to her maiden name after the war.'

Le Sauvage passed the paper over to Harris.

'You were right, Ted. She was a local girl. Her maiden name was Martel – and the child was a boy. Bernard! The question is, does he know? If so, that gives him a huge motive for getting rid of Richard'

* * *

In the small curtained-off alcove that contained the public telephone, Robbie made no movement or sound until the three policemen had left the lounge. Then he let out his breath in a sigh that was almost a sob, and fumbled with the telephone; frantic now to make the call to Hal that he had been about to dial when he had stopped to listen to the Inspector and the Sergeant. His breathing was rapid and irregular, and he muttered to himself in frustration as the phone rang and rang and nobody answered it.

'Come on, come on, Hal. Answer the bloody thing, can't you! You can't be out – not now ... Oh, hello, Mrs Lovering. It's Robbie here. Can I speak to Hal, please? ... Well, when will he be back? ... Yes, it is urgent, as a matter of fact – I really want to talk to him.'

The voice on the other end of the phone was concerned and anxious, and Robbie realised that he must be sounding hysterical. He made a real effort to control himself.

'No, really, Mrs Lovering, I'm quite all right. No, there's nothing you can do. Just tell Hal I called, please – and tell him ...'

His voice faltered, and he could only control the wobble in it by speaking much louder.

'Tell him I think the police are about to make an arrest!'

He couldn't trust himself to talk any more without breaking down altogether, so he put the receiver down and rushed out of the lounge, his eyes filling with tears so that he didn't recognise the person he just missed cannoning into on the way out.

# CHAPTER 20

The Inspector went to check on the possibility of getting a boat through the rapidly worsening weather to the mainland. Harris and Brouard were left waiting for him in the small bedroom at the top of the main staircase; it had been made available to them as an extra office space, to free the reception area for the hotel staff to carry on their work as normally as possible.

'The Inspector says he reckons he knows who did it,' said Harris conversationally. Brouard waited for him to continue, but no more was forthcoming.

'Well, aren't you going to tell me who?' he asked eventually, wondering uneasily if the Sergeant was waiting for him to work something out for himself.

Harris snorted.

'No, I'm not – and I'll tell you why; because I'm buggered if I know myself what he thinks, that's why! He's too crafty to commit himself to an actual name, and I'm too crafty to ask him for one, so I don't even know if he *does* suspect anyone in particular or if it's just one-upmanship. He wouldn't be the first Inspector to make his reputation by throwing out vague hints beforehand so that he can claim he knew who it was all along when the case eventually solves itself. As far as I can see at the moment, it could equally well be any one of three people. And that's just assuming the same person was responsible for both deaths.'

This bit the Constable felt he *was* capable of working out. It wasn't exactly difficult.

'It had to be someone who was on the boat, for Richard's death; that means Blythe, Martel or Mrs Taylor.'

Harris nodded.

'Assuming Martel was telling us the truth when he said there were only five of them on the boat to begin with.'

'And assuming it wasn't Abigail who did Richard in, and then jumped off the cliff herself in remorse.'

Harris looked at him in approval.

'Oh, well done! I wondered if you'd spot that. You'd be amazed how many people forget that a victim of one death can still be a suspect for another. I don't think that possibility has occurred to the Inspector, for a start, so award yourself a gold star for thinking of it. It's rather a pity the whole idea's a non-starter; it would be such a neat solution.'

'Why a non-starter?' asked Brouard, torn between pride in his idea and disappointment at the Sergeant's instant dismissal of it.

'It's no good having a theory that fits the facts if it doesn't fit the characters,' said Harris. 'Tell me honestly, can you make the idea of remorse match with the personality of that young lady? I can't – not in a million years.'

'I suppose not,' admitted Brouard reluctantly; then brightened. 'Hang on, though – it needn't have been suicide. Why do we have to have *two* suspicious deaths? What's wrong with simple accident for the second one? After all, that cliff path goes very near the edge, and it *was* foggy. That would leave us with just one killer, disposed of after the event by coincidence.'

'I don't believe in coincidence,' muttered Harris, 'Not in a murder investigation, I don't. In any case, what was she doing up there after dark, in the fog? Hardly the weather for a moonlight stroll, and she wasn't the type for that, anyway. And where's her motive for getting rid of Richard? We haven't even got a previous connection between them. No, it's much more likely to be the obvious; she saw whoever *did* do it, on the boat, and then saw the opportunity for a spot of blackmail. Now that *would* be in character. If so, the big question is, who did she see?'

'We can probably get a fair idea, once we've got everyone's detailed versions of what happened on board, can't we?'

'Oh yes, I don't doubt we can work it out eventually. But I tell you, Jim, the Inspector's right about one thing.'

'What's that, sir?'

'If we do arrive at a name, it will be a real sod to try and prove it.'

'Which of them do you think it is, sir?'

'I know which one of them I'd like it to be,' said Harris thoughtfully, 'but that's not quite the same thing. No, Jim – if the Inspector wouldn't tell me his favourite, I don't see why I should let you in on mine. Pick one for yourself. But I will tell you one thing I'm sure of ...'

'Yes, sir?'

'It all hinges on motive,' said Harris, as the door opened and the Inspector came in to collect them for the interview with Paul.

* * *

'Did you already know that you were Bernard's father?' asked Harris gently. He'd watched Paul's face closely as the Inspector went through the documentary evidence of Annette's marriage and the birth of her son. The old man had listened intently, but Harris couldn't decide whether he had shown any signs of surprise. Now Paul looked from Harris to Le Sauvage and back again, and a faint smile touched his lips.

'Not exactly,' he said, 'but I was beginning to suspect that I might be Robbie's grandfather. It seemed just an old man's fantasy at first, but then I began to see that it might very well be true. He's so like me, in so many ways. But the closer I came to believing it, the more reluctant I was to check Bernard's background and find out.'

'Because you didn't want it to be true?' asked Le Sauvage, and Harris wondered if the Inspector was being deliberately obtuse.

'Because I was afraid it might *not* be true,' said Paul. 'If it was an illusion, I wanted to leave it unshattered for as long as possible. I've grown amazingly fond of the boy in a very short time. It was cowardly of me, I suppose – but I didn't want to spoil the magic.'

* * *

Outside, the wind was angrily driving dark rain-clouds across the sky, and howling in a tantrum as it tore great handfuls of leaves off the trees and hurled them about in all directions. Robbie ran through the gathering storm, and his thoughts roared and rampaged with the wind. All the dark fears and suspicions he had so recently dispelled were crowding back in on him; they had just twisted round to point in a different direction. He saw now with a dreadful clarity that the motive he had half glimpsed for his mother could be reversed in the case of his father. The thoughts came piling in on top of him until his brain was spinning with the attempt to make sense of them; Richard's money, that his mother had thought safely out of reach with Richard's death, would now be available to Richard's brother – his father!

His world was collapsing around him; there was no magic in it after all; no safety, no comfort, nowhere to turn. His hiding place was just that; no real refuge, simply a place to run to when there was nowhere else to go. All the people he cared about betrayed him in the end – there was never anyone there when he really needed them.

He headed for the tunnel with the blind instinct of a hunted animal, and the wind howled after him like the horns of distant pursuers.

* * *

'You must have tried to find her yourself,' said the Inspector. 'We had no real difficulty tracing her – I would have thought you could have tracked her down when you were here ... when was it? It must have been the year that Muriel Wilson came to the island on honeymoon, soon after the war. You'd split up and lost touch with Annette – was that it? And then you came back to look for her.'

'It wasn't quite that simple, Inspector. The whole situation was chaotic immediately after the war – I doubt if I could have found her records then quite as easily as you did now. But I didn't actually try, in the end. You're quite right – I did intend to find her when I came back. But I changed my mind.'

'You mean you decided you didn't want to find her after all?'

'Oh no – I wanted to find her, all right. But I didn't think she wanted to be found. Especially once I knew the one fact I did establish from my search – that before she moved away to the mainland, there had been a child.'

Harris was puzzled.

'But surely that would make you *more* determined to find her, not less. With a child, there'd be even more reason to try to rescue the marriage. Wasn't that what you came to try to do?'

Paul smiled gently, and shook his head.

'Hardly, Sergeant. You see, there was no marriage – or not to me, at any rate.'

'But that's ridiculous,' protested Harris, ignoring the Inspector's warning frown, 'I've seen a copy of the marriage certificate.'

'I don't doubt it,' said Paul, 'but I was never married to Annette, all the same. She *was* married to Paul Taylor, but you see … I'm not Paul Taylor!'

# INTERLUDE : MARCH 1945

A thick pall of smoke hung over the still-burning shell of the guard room. Hugo picked his way through the ruins of the rest of the barracks with a heavy heart, knowing there was no real chance of finding anyone alive; it was likely that his men had all been together in the guard room, except for the single sentry on patrol. The sentry he already knew was beyond help; he'd found the body outside, the life crushed out of it by the falling stones of a collapsed wall. Little remained of the ammunition store itself, and the guard room had suffered badly because it was so close to the site of the main explosion. He moved slowly through the nightmare landscape of smoke and rubble, and felt numb; unable yet to grasp the full horror of what had happened.

At last he stumbled out into the open air, gasping for breath, his nostrils clogged with the stench of smoke and cordite and burned flesh. As he headed instinctively towards the causeway and the water to get away from the smoke, he remembered the other body. The figure he'd seen from the top of the cliff must have been struck by a piece of masonry hurled outwards by the force of the explosion; by the time

Hugo had reached the foot of the cliff and started to splash across the causeway to reach the fort, the figure was sprawled face downwards in a rocky pool beside the path. He'd paused only for long enough to convince himself the man must be dead before continuing his frantic rush to reach his men.

The body was still there; the water was rising slowly around it, and Hugo was seized with an irrational determination that it shouldn't be allowed to remain there to be swept away by the sea. He bent to grasp the shoulders, and dragged the body back along the causeway until he reached the grassy slope below what remained of the guard room. Panting with the effort, his lungs still full of smoke, he rolled over on the grass and gave himself up to coughing. When he turned back to the body beside him, his head was clearer and his thoughts were beginning to break through the numbness of shock.

He was sure now that the explosion had been sabotage, and equally sure that the body beside him was the saboteur, caught in his own trap; partly by his own incompetence in not leaving himself enough time to get clear, but also by the sheer bad luck of where the flying rubble fell.

The body still lay face down. Hugo was reluctant to turn it over, for as his thoughts continued to piece themselves together he became more and more sure of what he would find. At last he forced himself to kneel beside the body and roll it on to its back, and his suspicions were confirmed.

The face that gazed up into the smoke-filled air with fixed sightless eyes was that of Annette's husband, Paul.

* * *

It seemed to Hugo that he knelt there for a very long time, his thoughts in turmoil. So many things were slotting themselves into place, explaining incidents in the recent past: Annette's reluctance ever to talk to him about her husband, which he had thought stemmed from her own sense of guilt; the husband's frequent absences, supposedly on fishing trips; the fact that Annette had told him they had relations at St Saviour in Jersey, in the very parish where an ammunition dump and a Todt depot had both been sabotaged in the last week. He felt sick as he wondered how much she had known of her husband's activities; even sicker as he thought that she might even have helped him. He reminded himself that she had never asked him anything about the barracks or his duties there, but at the same time he remembered that their meeting tonight had been at her suggestion, not his. Had she known what was in store for the barracks, and engineered his absence? The feeling of sickness was still with him, but overlaid with a burning rage at the fate of his men.

He looked down at the body beside him, and for the first time recognised that it was wearing his own uniform jacket. His thoughts turned to the future. There would be an investigation; even in the difficulties and privations of this point in the war, with the Channel Islands cut off and abandoned, discipline had not yet become so slack that the Military Command on Guernsey would ignore an incident like this. He suddenly saw how dangerous his own position was; he had enemies enough on Guernsey to make sure he'd be called to account and asked to explain his own absence from the fort on the night of the sabotage, and God knew where that might end. In the dying stages of a war that was now clearly being lost, there were plenty of people looking for scapegoats, and plenty more with scores to settle.

He was not aware of taking a conscious decision, but he found himself lifting the corpse's feet to ease the legs out of their rough trousers, and unbuttoning his own uniform trousers.

As he continued with the grim task of changing clothes and identification papers with the corpse, he kept his mind firmly fixed on the physical detail of what he was doing, to prevent himself thinking of Annette. When he had finished, he dragged the body closer to the guard room and let it fall among the stones of a fallen section of wall, then he stepped back to look at the effect: a dead German officer in uniform, killed in the same explosion that had wiped out the entire garrison. With no survivors, the investigating group might well just bury the dead as soon as possible, and unless anyone in the party sent over from Guernsey knew him well enough to recognise him, the body would be accepted as his.

Satisfied, he turned to stride away; then hesitated and returned to kneel by the body for a moment. Gently he felt in the jacket pocket of the uniform and took out a small twist of paper. He opened out the paper and looked down at the delicate pink shell lying in his palm, then he folded it away into the paper again and transferred it to his own pocket.

He didn't look back at the fort as he waded through the steadily deepening water that was now covering the causeway, and climbed the cliff path, but at the top he turned and stood looking out over the beach to the open sea. He felt the tears well up in his eyes and spill over to trickle down his cheeks, as he was overwhelmed by an intense sense of loss. Such a short time had passed since he had stood on this same spot earlier in the evening, but within that time the world had changed utterly, and nothing could ever be the same again. He stood and wept; for Annette, for his men and for this magical island he had come to love and that he might never see again.

# CHAPTER 21

The storm raged on and Robbie raged with it, hurling his hurt away from him in howls of bitterness.

'Why me? How can you do this to me, Dad? It isn't fair! It isn't fair! It isn't bloody fair, and I hate you for it!'

The wind snatched the words from his mouth even as he formed them, and tossed them away through curtains of driving rain.

* * *

Harris was taking the notes this time, and he was having a hard time keeping up. Paul spoke fast and fluently – almost as if he were delivering a prepared statement he had learned by heart. The Sergeant thought the old man must have rehearsed this explanation over and over in his mind so many times, through the long years of keeping his secret, that the words flowed freely of their own accord. He wondered if Paul found their uttering at last a relief or a torment.

The Inspector was listening intently, taking the occasional note for his own benefit. Once or twice he glanced across at

Harris, as parts of the story tied in with what they already knew of Annette Taylor. But mostly he sat motionless, listening in astonishment as the man they knew as Paul Taylor recounted the story of Captain Hugo Von Essler, and how he had seized the opportunity to escape the horrors of war by taking a new identity.

Only towards the end of the story did Paul's voice falter, as he described the carnage he had found at the fort, and the terrible shock of realising that the man responsible for the death of his men was Annette's husband.

'She swore she'd known nothing of what he was planning – and I did believe her. But I knew that there would always be one small part of my mind that felt it was possible she'd lied, even to me, and that meant that nothing could ever be the same between us again. She knew that, too – I could tell she felt it as keenly as I did. That was why I didn't try too hard to find her, when I came back later. I felt that if she wanted to be found – if she'd been able to put the past behind her – she would have left me some clue. But there was nothing.'

'She moved away from the island soon after the baby was born, as far as we can tell from the information we have so far,' said the Inspector. 'She registered his place of birth as Longuey, but she used her maiden name of Martel. She went to Guernsey and found her father's sister, who took her in and cared for them both until Bernard was old enough to go to school.'

Paul sighed.

'Yes, I see. Of course, it's what she would have done. I never knew her maiden name. If I did, I might have traced her in spite of my misgivings, all those years ago, and perhaps I could have made her change her mind, and everything would have been different.

'I don't believe she ever really loved him, you know. They

stayed together because of the farm, and the herd; it was a strong enough bond in its way, but she never loved him. Not the way she loved me. Their marriage was over before I met her; half-way over even before the war destroyed what was left of it. I gave her love, and I gave her a son, but she wouldn't come with me, not then. The horror of it was too close. The horror, and the guilt. I tried to persuade her. I really thought we could leave the war behind us, and make a new life together – Mr and Mrs Paul Taylor. But she wouldn't listen. She kept crying, and babbling about names. 'Can't you see, Hugo? I can't take yours, and I won't keep Paul's. Neither of them would be honest, now.' She didn't know she was pregnant, then, but I can see why when the time came she felt the only name she could give her son was one that belonged to her alone. She was always alone from then on. And in a way, God help me, so was I.'

* * *

Outside the door, Sarah Taylor hesitated with her hand on the door-handle. The two policemen had politely but firmly rejected her offer to stay with Paul while they questioned him, but suggested that she should stay within earshot in case he became agitated. That had been some time ago, and she had half expected to be called in; she could hear the murmur of voices through the door now, but it was impossible to make out any words.

She stood motionless for a long time, listening, then dropped her hand to her side and straightened her shoulders, and went upstairs to her room. She didn't seem to be needed here after all, and there was a letter she had to write.

* * *

Time passed, and the storm wound itself up to a peak of fury, finally bursting out with sizzles of lightning and almost simultaneous thunderclaps. Robbie, crouched in the chamber at the end of the tunnel in a huddle of pure misery, looked out over the raging sea and saw the lightning flashes without any reaction; normally he hated thunderstorms, but now he was far beyond fear or feeling; unaware even of how wet and cold he was.

It was only when he felt the whole tunnel shake that he came far enough back to life to feel fear, and by then it was too late – the huge tree that came crashing down at the height of the storm completely blocked the entrance to the tunnel, and he was trapped.

* * *

Time passed, and the voices behind the closed door continued their murmurings as Paul's statement was read back to him. Sarah, her letter finished, came downstairs and stopped to listen briefly at the door as she crossed the hall. Then she opened the front door and slipped out into the full force of the storm that raged outside.

* * *

The interview completed, Harris and Le Sauvage left Paul temporarily in the care of the woman constable, and considered their next move.

'It's an amazing story, all right,' said the Inspector, 'but the question is – does it change anything?'

'Only if anyone else knew about it. I don't really see how they could; he's only told us because he felt he had to explain about Annette.'

'Could be someone else who put him in the same position, I suppose. We didn't find it too difficult to track down the birth – what if somebody found out and approached Paul in much the same way we did? Would he have come out with the whole story, do you think?'

Harris considered, then shook his head.

'No – I think he was telling it for the first time to us just now; you could feel the effort it cost him to begin, and then the relief as he got into the flow of it. Anyway, the German connection is irrelevant, surely, fascinating though it is. It doesn't really change anything about the child, and the inheritance. And even they may turn out to be red herrings in the end. I have a feeling that money is only indirectly important in this case. The real motive is elsewhere – and I think I could hazard a guess where we should look first. Classic principles pay off in this case: process of elimination, for one, and remembering the most likely suspect, for another.'

Le Sauvage nodded reluctantly.

'I know.'

'Been putting it off, haven't we?' said Harris gloomily. 'Well – we can't really put it off any longer.'

'This is one interview I'm not looking forward to at all, Ted.'

'You and me both, sir,' sighed Harris, as they headed for the stairs, 'you and me both.'

# CHAPTER 22

The letter they found on Sarah Taylor's dressing table was addressed to Sergeant Harris. He held it out to the Inspector, but Le Sauvage shook his head.

'You'd better open it, Ted; that's obviously what she wanted. If it's what we think it is, I'll get to read it soon enough.'

With a certain amount of reluctance, Harris opened the envelope and began to read. After a few sentences, he looked up at the Inspector and nodded without speaking. Le Sauvage sighed.

'A full confession?'

'Looks like it, sir. She must have known we'd come to interview her after Blythe and Martel, as the only other remaining person who was on the boat at the time. And so we would have done, if the bombshell about Paul hadn't got in the way. That gave her time to pre-empt us, and write this.'

'Classic principles, all right, Ted. Look for the close relative, usually the spouse. I told you not to be too quick to give up on the domestic angle, didn't I, right at the beginning.'

'Domestic motives are always the strongest,' agreed

Harris mechanically, reading on. There was no sense of satisfaction at a successful conclusion to the case; all he felt was an overwhelming sadness as he read Sarah's words, wondering all the time why she should have addressed them specifically to him.

'I really didn't mean the girl to die. It's important to me that you understand that, Sergeant; I don't quite know why, but it is. I would have paid her what she asked for, you see. I didn't see any need to harm her.

'I knew as soon as she asked to talk to me that morning that she'd be after money. I didn't know then about Paul's will, and the problems it might cause with the money, so it seemed quite straightforward – pay her off with a lump sum, in return for her silence about what she'd seen on the boat and a promise not to contact me again. But I knew I had to be firm with her when I met her in the evening to pay her off, or it wouldn't have stopped there. She was a greedy little bitch; she would have come back for more. I had to convince her I wouldn't stand any more of her demands in the future, so I shouted at her. We were standing quite close together, at the edge of the cliff. I got angry and really screamed right in her face. She was startled – I don't think she'd expected me to fight back – and she backed away from me and slipped. We hadn't realised in the fog that we'd drifted so far off the path. Before I could do anything to stop her, she'd gone over the edge.

'I heard her screaming all the way down. I can hear her now.

'I didn't know whether she'd said anything about her suspicions to anyone else. I hoped that if I kept quiet, everyone would assume it was just an unfortunate accident in the fog. As indeed it was.

'I don't feel guilty, or even particularly sorry, about

Abigail; she was a vicious, self-seeking little schemer. But I do feel guilty about Richard. I did mean to kill him, you see. It wasn't planned beforehand, but when it happened I really meant it.

'He was drunk. We'd all had a few too many, but Richard was really high; excited at the prospect of making a lot of money. I went out on deck, and Richard was there, stumbling about and muttering to himself. I asked him about Paul – what would happen now about the provisions for him to go into residential care. He laughed in my face. He told me the money would all be tied up in the island consortium, and there wouldn't even be enough left to pay for a private nurse at home.

'You'll just have to do it all yourself, old girl,' he said, and he was still laughing as he said it. 'You managed with your mother, didn't you? You can just do it all over again for Dad. Good old Sarah. Whatever would I do without you?'

'In that moment I saw the rest of my life disappearing into a dreary purgatory of caring for Paul, without an ounce of support from Richard. I knew I hated him then. I would have tried to kill him with my bare hands, but he saved me the trouble. He saw the look on my face, and sobered up instantly. He put his hands out to ward me off as I came at him, and backed away, and then he lost his footing and he was over the side.

'I've tried to remember ever since – when I got the brush, did I intend to help him back on board? He grabbed at it, and I could have held him there and yelled for help.

'Instead, I pushed him under, and tried to keep him under.

'It seemed to take for ever. He was struggling and thrashing about, and I was pushing his head back under every time it broke the surface. He's not a strong swimmer, and the drink can't have helped. The struggles got weaker and eventually stopped, and he went under and didn't come straight back up again.

'I regretted it immediately when I realised what I'd done. I shouted for help, then put the brush back and went for the lifebelt. By the time I threw it, Richard had surfaced again, but he was unconscious. Abigail arrived on deck almost as soon as I shouted. She must have seen me with the brush, and realised the significance of that when the marks on the face were mentioned at the inquest.

'You probably know the rest by now. or you can piece it together for yourself. We hauled him out, but we couldn't revive him. Neville and Bernard organised the cover-up. All I had to do was give Bernard a set of Richard's clothes, but in the panic we both forgot to include shoes. The clothes we took off Richard's body are back in his wardrobe now; the hotel has an excellent washing machine available to guests at all hours of the day or night. By the time I'd finished washing them that night, Paul was having one of his bad turns and I had to sit up with him. I didn't mind – I couldn't possibly have slept anyway.

'I haven't slept very much since. It doesn't make any difference; sleeping or waking, I have the same picture inside my head. I shall never be able to forget the look of terror on Richard's face, and his fingers scrabbling at the brush as he went under that last time. That is my punishment, and I know it will stay with me for the rest of my life. The only choice I have left to me now is to reduce the length of that life sentence.

'I'm sorry about Paul. He'll just have to become somebody else's problem now. It's ironic, really – that was what I was trying to ensure all along, I suppose, but I didn't intend to achieve it quite like this.'

* * *

Harris looked up at Le Sauvage with a combination of urgency and hopelessness.

'We'll have to get a search started at once.'

'She won't get far, not in this weather.'

'Oh, I don't think she wants to get far,' said Harris wearily, handing the letter over to the Inspector. 'She must know we'll find her soon enough. She just doesn't want us to find her alive.'

* * *

The first stage of the search for Sarah, checking systematically on all the rooms in the hotel, threw up an additional problem. Robbie too had disappeared.

The Inspector and the Sergeant met again in the front hall, as the first group of searchers gathered to don waterproof clothing before going out into the storm that still raged outside.

'We haven't got enough men,' said Le Sauvage anxiously. 'This bloody weather is all we needed. I can contact the mainland, but there's no way they can send anyone over. Martel says there's no possibility of a boat being able to get through to land here with this combination of wind and tides. A search outside would be difficult enough anyway in a storm like this, but with just the team that came over this morning it will be a nightmare trying to cover all the ground.'

'We can use Martel and the staff of the hotel to help, surely?' said Harris. 'Now we've got Sarah's confession, it's not as if anyone else is under suspicion. Well – except for the attempt at a cover-up, of course, but that's hardly in the same league as murder, is it?'

The Inspector looked doubtful.

'It's not going by the book, Ted.'

'Bugger the book, sir!' said Harris quietly. 'Quite apart from Sarah, this is a boy's life we may be talking about here. And the person who knows the island best is Martel. We need him, right now; let's find Sarah and the boy first, and you can throw the book at him afterwards if you still think it's necessary'

Le Sauvage made up his mind.

'O.K. Ted – you're right, of course. We'll need to organise everyone we can to join the search, while there's still some light left. I'll leave that to you to get started. I've got something to do first. Someone has to go and break the news to Paul.'

Harris half opened his mouth to offer to go with him, then closed it again. There were some occasions when it was a relief and a blessing to know that responsibility rested with someone else.

* * *

In the hiding place that had now turned into a trap, Robbie was just beginning to get really frightened. The falling tree had crashed into the mouth of the tunnel with sufficient force to bring down a section of the roof, and there was no way he could possibly find a way through the tangle of rocks and earth and root and branch that now blocked the entrance; it would take men with shovels to dig him out. But to do that, they would need to know he was there.

He wondered how long it would be before anyone even noticed that he was missing, and how long after that before they were worried enough to start looking for him. Meanwhile, he was already wet through and getting colder by the minute, and the light would begin to fade soon. He knew enough from scout expeditions to be seriously worried about hypothermia; he found himself wondering what his chances were, without dry clothing or any real protection from the cold, of surviving until the next morning.

The wind from the sea was whipping into the opening in the cliff-face, and blowing salt spray into the chamber at the end of the tunnel. Robbie was reluctant to leave the sight of the open air and face the claustrophobia of the narrower end of the tunnel, but he knew his best chance of discovery would be there. He went back to the blocked entrance and found what shelter he could from the freezing draught, burrowing into a niche between a huge branch and some fallen rocks. At least there was no danger of running out of oxygen, he thought, as he settled down to try to conserve his energy. From time to time he shouted, and the playful wind waited outside the tunnel mouth to catch his voice and blow it away.

* * *

Le Sauvage had heard about Paul Taylor's strange catatonic states; he wondered if this might be the beginning of one, as the old man stared at him without speaking or moving or even blinking. He wasn't sure how much of what he'd been saying Paul had actually taken in; after one first sharp intake of breath and clenching of his fingers there had been no further reaction at all, just this dreadful blankness. The Inspector looked helplessly at the woman police constable who sat at Paul's side, and wondered if he ought to begin all over again. He walked over to the window and signed to her to follow. When she joined him, he spoke just above a whisper.

'Did he understand all that, do you think? I'm worried

about him – he's had a very traumatic day already, and I'm not sure how he's reacting. Perhaps we should have postponed telling him about Sarah.'

She shook her head.

'I don't think so, sir. I was talking to him earlier, after you interviewed him, and he seemed quite normal then – tired, yes, but not really traumatised. I think it was a relief to him to have told his story at last. And the way he is now – well, it's nothing like the state he was in when we told him about Richard's death. I think this is just a fairly normal shock reaction. He'll come out of it in his own good time.'

'Perhaps,' muttered Le Sauvage doubtfully. 'I wish we had the doctor here, all the same.'

'He'll be all right. I'll stay with him, and Mrs Martel will probably come and give me a hand if I ask her.'

Le Sauvage frowned, and forgot to keep his voice low.

'No – better not ask Mrs Martel. She'll be worried about the boy. She may even want to come out and join in the search for him.'

'Robbie?'

The voice was Paul's. They went back to his chair, and saw with relief that the spell was broken; he was fully aware of his surroundings again, and though there was anxiety in his tone there was no hysteria.

'You said a search – is the boy missing, too?'

'Yes,' said Le Sauvage, 'but there's no need to worry. We'll soon find him, I'm sure. We'll have plenty of people out looking for him, and he can't have gone far on an island this small.'

He turned and headed for the door.

'No need for you to fret about Robbie,' soothed the constable, 'I'm sure he'll soon be back safe and sound.'

She laid a comforting hand on Paul's shoulder, but he brushed it away angrily and struggled to his feet.

'I must help!' he said urgently.

'No, no,' said Le Sauvage, turning back towards him, 'There's nothing you can do, and we'll let you know as soon as we find him.'

'You don't understand,' said Paul, and his voice was strong and confident. 'I'm not offering to come and join the search, but you do need my help all the same. You see – I think I know where he'll have gone!'

* * *

The cold had gone beyond the stage where it was a burden, and the numbness in Robbie's limbs was almost beginning to feel pleasant. He fought against drowsiness, knowing that he must try to stay conscious so that he could go on shouting, but the temptation to drift into sleep was getting harder and harder to resist. The cold was doing odd things to his thought processes, too – he found he was no longer worried at all, about anything. He could hardly remember now what any of his suspicions had been about, and he was certain that if only he could get out of this place and be back home with his parents – both his parents – then there would never be anything to worry about ever again. He'd just snuggle deep under the bedclothes to get warm, and when he woke the next morning everything would be all right.

'Robbie!'

It was too early to get up yet. Why couldn't they just leave him in peace for a few more minutes?

'Robbie! Are you in there, Robbie?'

He struggled to open his eyes, then made one enormous effort to shout, as he recognised the voice outside.

'Dad!'

There were more voices, and then a long confusion of movement and noise and flickering torchlight getting steadily nearer. At last he felt strong hands lift him and carry him out into the open, and a burly figure that he recognised as the Sergeant who had first questioned him rushed forward to wrap a blanket round him.

Blinking in the torchlight and gasping as the wind and rain stung his cheeks, he looked round for the two figures he knew would be there together – and found them.

'Thank God!' said Bernard, and tightened his grip around Claire's waist as she buried her head in his shoulder and wept with relief.

By the time they had taken Robbie back to the hotel it was too late and too dark to continue the search for Sarah; it was not until the next morning, at first light in the eerily quiet calm after the storm, that they found her body at the foot of the same cliff where Abigail had fallen.

# EPILOGUE

'It all worked out quite neatly in the end, when you come to think about it, didn't it, sir?' said Brouard cheerfully.

'Depends what you mean by neatly,' grunted Harris, making heavy weather of his end of an exercise bicycle. 'One death too many, for a start. Confession followed by suicide isn't exactly my favourite way of ending a case. We should have got on to her sooner, only we let too many complications get in the way.'

'Probably all for the best, though.'

'Maybe, Jim. I don't know. It would certainly have been a difficult trial, and a terrible strain on Paul. I suppose that was what she wanted to avoid.'

'The Inspector's pleased there's no need for a trial, anyway,' said Brouard, as they manoeuvred along the corridor and back into the incident room.

Harris snorted, and let his end of the bicycle drop with a bump.

'You bet he is! It gets the bigwigs off his back. Leaves a nasty taste in my mouth though – that slimy bastard Blythe sliding out from under most of the trouble.'

'He did get a caution, sir.'

'Bet he didn't exactly get his knuckles properly rapped, though. It will have been all sweetness and light and "remember me to the Commissioner when you next see him". Still, he didn't get off entirely scot-free, I'm happy to say.'

Brouard looked at the Sergeant shrewdly, noting the satisfaction in his face.

'It wouldn't have been you that tipped off that hack from the "News of the World", would it, by any chance?'

'Who, me?' said Harris innocently. 'Perish the thought! Anyway, those muckrakers don't need tips from the likes of you and me. I don't know quite how they do it, but they can sniff out trouble all on their own.'

He led the way back to the store-room in silence, and only continued when he'd closed the door behind them.

'No, Jim, I didn't spill a dickey bird about Blythe to the gentlemen of the press – but I did take the trouble to look up the address of his wife.'

Brouard looked puzzled.

'But surely the press had already contacted her – she must have ended up knowing as much as they did about Abigail.'

Harris grinned.

'About Abigail, yes. But the press didn't have access to all Martel's *previous* registers, did they? I just thought she might be entitled to know who he was with last year – and the year before that!'

Brouard whistled.

'So that's why she didn't do the standard act of standing by him.'

'Serves him right!' said Harris calmly, bending to roll up a floor-mat. 'The man's a snake – she's better off without him.'

They worked in silence for a while, until all the floormats were neatly rolled. Then Harris spoke again.

'You're right, of course. It has worked out quite neatly. A crime cleared up without need for a trial, and a decision not to prosecute anyone for the cover-up. However much I disapprove of the reason for that decision, I'm glad it worked out like that for Martel – and especially for the boy.'

'It's amazing, really, how it turned out – Paul being Robbie's grandfather. It could all end up quite well in the end.'

Harris sighed, and looked at the constable in fond exasperation.

'They all lived happily ever after – is that it?'

'Well – it could be something like that sir, yes,' said Brouard, unabashed. 'It looks as if the Martels are back together again, now that the scheme for that awful marina complex has been scotched. And surely the obvious thing to happen would be for Paul to live with them and use his money to develop the island sensibly. He obviously adores the boy, and he seems to have come through the shock of Sarah's death surprisingly well. Perhaps all he really needs now is a new family.'

'You know the trouble with you, Jim? You're an incurable romantic!'

Brouard hoisted a pile of mats on to his shoulder.

'I know, sir. Whereas you ...'

'I'm a realist!' said Harris, staggering after him with the rest of the mats.

'All the same, lad,' he muttered as he struggled to close the door behind him, 'I hope to God you're right!'

# ACKNOWLEDGEMENTS

The island of Longuey and the characters in this book are my own invention, and no resemblance is intended with real people or places. But anyone who knows the Channel Islands will recognise my huge debt to the island of Herm. This magical island has saved my sanity and refreshed my spirit over the course of many holiday visits over the years, and was the main inspiration for the writing of this book. My thanks in particular go to Adrian and Penny Heywood and their staff, and Chief Inspector LePage from the Guernsey police.

Printed in Great Britain
by Amazon

28051069R00128